EXPLODING ENDINGS

Books by Tim Harris

Exploding Endings 1: Painted Dogs & Doom Cakes
Exploding Endings 2: Dingbats & Lollypop Arms
Exploding Endings 3: Cursed Pants & Cranky Cops
Exploding Endings 4: Screenshots & Laughing Gas

Mr Bambuckle's Remarkables
Mr Bambuckle's Remarkables Fight Back
Mr Bambuckle's Remarkables Go Wild
Mr Bambuckle's Remarkables On the Lookout

Toffle Towers 1: Fully Booked
Toffle Towers 2: The Great River Race
Toffle Towers 3: Order in the Court

timharrisbooks.com

EXPLODING ENDINGS

Dingbats & Lollypop Arms

TIM HARRIS

PUFFIN BOOKS

PUFFIN BOOKS

UK | USA | Canada | Ireland | Australia
India | New Zealand | South Africa | China

Penguin
Random House
Australia

Penguin Random House Australia is part of the Penguin Random House group of companies whose addresses can be found at global.penguinrandomhouse.com.

First published by Harbour Publishing House in 2016
This edition published by Puffin Books, an imprint of
Penguin Random House Australia Pty Ltd, in 2020

Typeset by Harbour Publishing House.
Additional typesetting changes by Midland Typesetters, Australia.

Printed and bound in Australia by Griffin Press, an accredited
ISO AS/NZS 14001 Environmental Management Systems printer

NATIONAL LIBRARY OF AUSTRALIA

A catalogue record for this book is available from the National Library of Australia

ISBN 978 1 76 089802 1

Penguin Random House Australia uses papers that are natural and recyclable products, made from wood grown in sustainable forests. The logging and manufacture processes are expected to conform to the environmental regulations of the country of origin.

penguin.com.au

CONTENTS

FOR PETE & RUTH

THE TOP 79 EXCUSES FOR TALKING IN CLASS

1. Our conversation was revolving around your lovely haircut. Who does your fringe?

2. We are broadcasting a live podcast. Please stop interrupting.

3. You must be hearing things again. I'm always impressed by your keen sense of imagination. It inspires me to write made-up stories.

4. It's just that you enthuse us so much. We can't help but bubble over into joyous reflection.

5. I had to tell Darren that the world was about to end. Looks like I was wrong. Again. *look at

Darren and give a massive sigh of relief* *again*

6. My shadow made me do it.

7. It wasn't me. My mouth may have been moving, but that's because I was singing along to a song in my head. Sometimes I do that to help me concentrate.

8. I've gotta hand it to you. You're good. You're very, very good. I'll let the other teachers know what a high standard you set. I'm back with you now. So, what were you saying?

9. I was just making verbal notes about your wonderful lesson.

10. We weren't really talking. We were just pretending.

11. I'm raising money for charity by speaking all day long. Would you like to sponsor me?

12. You'd be talking, too, if you'd just found out your parents were actually dolphins.

13. I just won a small part in a movie. I was awarded the role of a school student who is always speaking in class. I'm just getting into character. I'm pretty good, hey?

14. I'm actually an undercover FBI agent. Don't ask any more questions or this could get serious. *put sunglasses on and continue to speak to your friend in a hushed tone*

15. 'Silence, kids'? We thought you said, 'silence kills'.

16. What you heard was actually the class next door. Kids these days…

17. It was a private conversation but, if you must know, Stephanie has decided to stop dancing lessons because she has uneven toes. Happy?

18. It's a long story. It all started on the way to school when I discovered that rhinoceros tusks are made

of keratin. Keratin is like hair! It's pretty much the same as hair? A rhino's horn is hair?! Now do you understand why I was speaking in class?

19. I'm not one for excuses, but my tongue just started talking all by itself. Honestly, I was powerless to stop it. *look emotionally fragile*

20. I wasn't talking, I was creating poetry. You make me so happy.

21. So, it's okay for you to keep talking? Whatever happened to equality? Child rights? My mouth is my prism.

22. Sorry, I was just clearing my throat and it sounded like words.

23. 'Quiet please'? I thought you said, 'choir police'. You need to be clearer about these things. By the way, was I in tune?

24. Every time you tell me to stop talking, a dolphin dies. Grow a heart.

25. It was the butler! *politely ask your teacher if they have ever played Cluedo*

26. I have a sore throat and I was giving it some

warm-up exercise. The doctor told me I need to speak for at least 30 minutes a day. I was going to do it at lunch, but eating is important.

27. Have you ever seen that film *Back to the Future*? *wait for teacher to talk about what a great film it is. This is called a tangent and is welcomed warmly by most teachers. You're off the hook*

28. I'm not sorry at all. I really like speaking to my friends and you need to understand that this is a high priority for me. Teach you may, but talk I must!

29. Did I ever tell you what a great listener you are?

30. I had to call an urgent meeting with my friends about some playground stuff that is going on. It's a bit private, so if you don't mind…

51. I'm so sorry. I thought this was a dream and there were no consequences.

52. Dare me to keep talking?

53. It all started yesterday when you asked us to discuss the latest ideas on global warming. I haven't stopped thinking about it. I also haven't stopped talking about it.

54. I have to talk, otherwise my tongue will freeze. Could you please turn the heater on?

55. The kids in the older classes said you wouldn't mind. See me later and I'll give you their names. They are bad news, those kids. Bad news all the way. *shake head disapprovingly*

36. There is a hairball caught in my throat. Literally. There is actually one wedged in my windpipe. That's the last time I try licking my cat clean. I'll leave it to Fluffy next time.

37. I'm translating the lesson into Mandarin. *Xie xie.*

38. Hang on a sec, I'm just finishing this conversation… *finish speaking to friend* Okay, what was it you wanted to ask me?

39. It's really important. Can the lesson wait?

40. Oh no, we weren't talking. We were listening… to each other! Bahahahahaha!!

41. I've got an itch in my throat, and the only way to scratch it is to talk.

42. I'm experimenting with the latest speech pathology techniques. But you wouldn't know anything about that because you're just a teacher. Maybe you should have concentrated harder at university.

43. I had to ask George a question. *look at George and ask him why he hates the teacher. This will take all the focus away from you and get George into trouble* *avoid George for the rest of the year*

44. I'm practising for the public-speaking competition. How was I? I can speak louder if you like. How was the eye contact and general delivery? I get so nervous at these events. Was my articulation all right?

45. 'Listen here'? I thought you said, 'lessen air'. I was finding it hard to breathe!

46. I'm a rapper, man! Talkety do wap woo!

47. Sorry, would you like us to take this outside?

48. I thought you said there should only be one person speaking at a time. That's a bit rich – you coming in and talking over the top of our chat. Hyp. O. Crite.

49. Would we be in more trouble if we told you we were speaking about your new dress? We're not sure that shade of green goes with your shoes.

50. You'd want to talk, too, if your shares just went up 250%. How much would it cost to get me off detention?

51. It's not me. I swallowed my iPod and it's blurting out of my mouth.

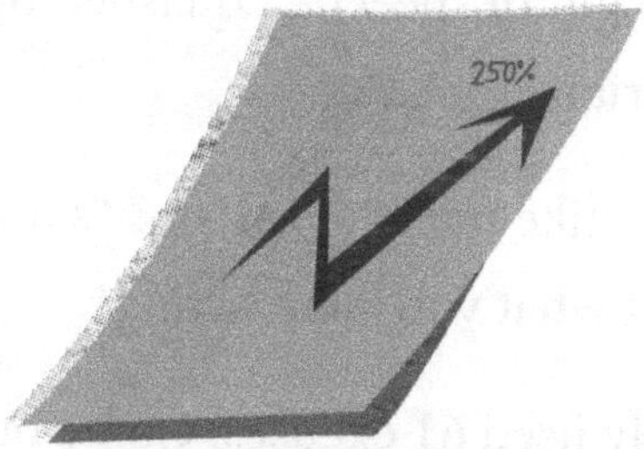

52. Can we make a deal? I'll agree not to talk if you do as well.

53. I'm terribly sorry. How rude of us not to include you. Do pull up a chair and join us. You'll never guess who Zoe likes!

54. Mum wanted me to participate more actively in lessons.

55. The real issue here is your eavesdropping.

56. I was brushing my teeth with soundwaves. Hygiene at its finest.

57. Tim Harris made me do it.

58. I was simply trying to increase my vocabulary. I've just added 'boring' and 'lesson' to my swag.

59. 'No more noise'? I thought you said, 'know your noise'.

60. Ahhh, the gift of speech… quashed by yet another disciplinarian.

61. Would you like me to speak up? *stand on desk and repeat what you were saying*

62. I've already used 61 excuses. Come on – just give me a break!

63. I said, 'Please don't let anyone know about the wart on my big toe!' Thanks for ruining my life, sir.

64. I never did have good manners. You should see me at the dinner table.

65. We've been talking for about 15 minutes! Ha! How slow are you?!

66. There's a sticky patch under my desk and we're just trying to get to the bottom of it. Looks like those high schoolers have been chewing gum again, while we've been chewing the fat! Get it?! Ha!

67. It's National Speaking Day. Well done, you're fitting right in!

68. I can text the rest of the conversation if you like?

That'd be quieter, right? Can I get my phone off your desk?

69. I was just trying to recite everything you were saying. *look at teacher and give an adoring smile*

70. We were just discussing how wonderful the Exploding Endings books are. Surely that's a good excuse, right? Oh, 100 house points. Why, thank you very much. What's your favourite book in the series, if you don't mind me asking? Yeah, I know what you mean – it's hard to have a favourite when they're all incredible.

71. I wasn't talking. I was praying. That bit of roof directly above your head looks loose again. I won't tell you which way I was praying…

72. It was a ghost. A very… audible… ghost.

73. We were just recording our voices on Sam's phone. Would you like to hear the playback at super-slow speed? Freeeeeaaaaaaky!

74. I'll be quiet next time. I promise. I really don't talk that much. See what I mean? I'm pretty good when I want to be. I'm not even speaking now. I can be so good when I absolutely have to be. I mean, look at me now – as quiet as a mouse. I'm, like, totally silent here. Ain't got nothin' comin' outta these little lips… this is a problem, isn't it?

75. I'm addicted to words.

76. It's just that I want to be a teacher one day. I'm practising what I would say if it was my lesson. You give me dreams I can run with.

77. We were just quoting famous movie lines. You've gotta admit, that's pretty darn fun to do!

78. I was just chewing really loudly.

79. Oh no... you must understand... we were simply planning your farewell party. There will be cake, drinks, chocolate and some speeches. These things take a lot of active discussion. On another note, how long have you been having a nervous breakdown for?

SWEET TOOTH SEAGULL

ONE

'Lara! Don't feed the seagulls!'

Dad was cross.

'But it's just the crumbs,' I replied. That was my first lie. I had actually thrown away a perfectly good chip. A chip covered in tomato sauce. And chicken salt. A chip Dad would love to have eaten. He always wanted more.

'Then what do you call that?' he asked, pointing to the tomato-sauced, chicken-salt chip, which was now lying in the sand.

'Dinner for two,' I said, as a couple of seagulls moved in on the action. 'Jaz threw that there,' I added. That was my second lie.

'Did not!' protested my younger sister. 'Mitch put it there!' She turned to look at my toddler brother. He was always in trouble. Usually for stuff that Jaz and I did. We were good at blaming him. Actually, I was good at blaming Jaz and she was good at blaming Mitch.

Dad took away the rest of Mitch's chips. 'No more for you then,' he said firmly. Mitch started crying. Silly Mitch.

'Ahhh, this is the life,' said Dad, turning to look at the ocean. 'Come on, kids, stop mucking around and enjoy the scenery. Smell the salty air. Look at the waves, the sand, the birds. Isn't it great?'

'It sure is,' said Mum, who had just come back from

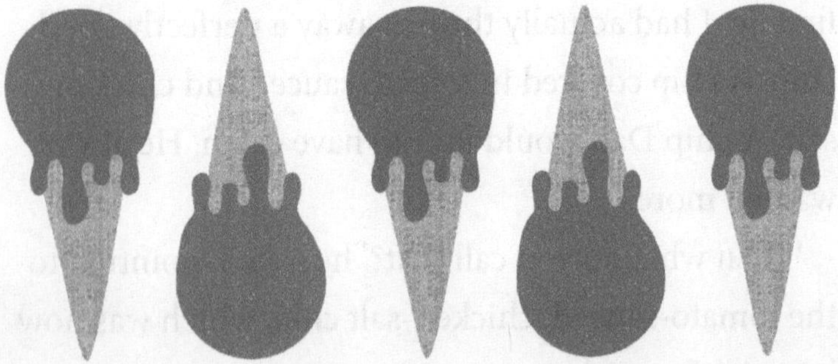

the shops with our ice creams. 'Now, who wanted chocolate?'

Mum was holding five ice-cream cones between her hands. Our family is crazy about ice cream. There is always plenty of it at home. Sometimes, Dad gets cranky because there is never room for anything else in the freezer. I think Mum gives in to Mitch's tantrums when they go shopping together. She always comes back with more ice cream when she goes shopping with Mitch. Silly Mitch.

'I wanted chocolate,' I said. That was my third lie. I had actually asked for vanilla, but seeing how big Mitch's chocolate ice cream was, I changed my mind. Mum handed me the chocolate ice cream and gave the vanilla one to Mitch.

Mum and Dad took us to the beach every summer. Every year, without fail, we would go. It was our favourite place. Mum loved swimming in the ocean water, Jaz loved making castles in the sand, Dad loved reading books on the sand and Mitch loved eating the sand.

Me, I loved the seagulls. I loved watching them and I loved feeding them. I loved their bright, white feathers and their red beaks and legs. I loved how they flew around the beach looking for something to eat. Whenever we had lunch at the beach, I always saved some of my food for them. The seagulls were my friends and I had to feed them. I think they liked me, too – Lara, the girl who fed her feathered friends.

Dad was too busy eating his strawberry ice cream to notice me borrow the rest of Mitch's confiscated chips. When I say borrow, you know what I mean, right? I quietly pulled the half-eaten carton of chips away from Dad and hid them next to my leg. Then, whenever he wasn't watching, I flung a chip out onto the sand for the seagulls. Soon, a small crowd of gulls had gathered.

'Now, where did they come from?' sighed Dad. I don't know why he didn't like the seagulls, but he was always growling at them and telling us not to feed them. 'Ssshhhooo! Get away, pesky birds!' he huffed, waving his arms over his head like a helicopter. This made the ice cream fall out of his cone. When I say fall, I mean slingshot. It landed with a splat in the sand. Everyone except Dad laughed. Mitch laughed so hard that his ice cream fell out of his cone, too. Silly Mitch.

'Look,' said Mum. 'One of the birds wants to eat it.' She was right. A small seagull with dark spots on its chest had landed near Dad's spilt ice cream. It looked down at the strawberry mess

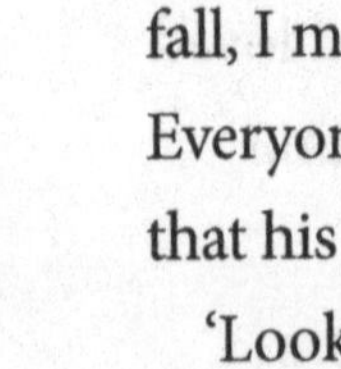

and nodded slowly, as if deciding it was good to eat. It started pecking at the ice cream, opening its beak every now and then to suck some in. It seemed to enjoy the taste and quickly finished gulping down the dessert before fluttering over to Mitch. Mitch screamed and dived headfirst into the sand. I don't think he liked seagulls. Dad had probably made him scared of them with all of his fussing. Anyway, the seagull ignored the ostrich toddler and started pecking away at the spilt vanilla ice cream. It made light work of its second dessert and then simply flew away.

'How strange,' said Mum. 'A sweet-toothed seagull.'

TWO

The sweet-toothed seagull was at the beach the next day, too. It was the final morning of our trip before we had to head home. Mum and Dad decided that lunch at the beach would be a good way to finish off the trip. We were eating salad rolls (of which I was quite happy to donate most of mine to the seagulls) when I first noticed the bird. The dark spots on its

chest gave it away.

'Look, Jaz,' I whispered to my sister. 'It's that funny seagull from yesterday.'

The small bird stood still on the sand, watching the other seagulls fighting over my salad roll.

'Maybe it only likes sweet things,' suggested Jaz. 'That's why it's not going for the roll.'

'Maybe,' I said. 'Oh wait, look!'

The seagull puffed out its spotted chest and then nodded slowly, as if to say the salad roll was good to eat. It then barged the other gulls out of the way, picked up the roll in its beak and swallowed it down in one gulp.

'Lara!' gasped Jaz. 'Did you see that?'

'Yes,' said Dad, who had also seen. 'And which naughty child threw their lunch to the birds?'

'Jaz,' I replied quickly.

'Mitch,' said Jaz just as quickly.

Luckily for us, Mitch had buried his salad roll in the sand and his hands were empty. He was probably imagining himself as a pirate and had buried his treasure. Either that or he wanted to turn his roll into a *real* sandwich! Get it? Anyway, Dad wasn't impressed.

'No dessert for you then,' he said, frowning at Mitch.

Silly Mitch.

I spent most of lunch watching Sweet Tooth. That was its name, I'd decided – Sweet Tooth. Though, strangely, it didn't seem so small now. The day before, it had seemed much smaller than the other birds. I thought my eyes were playing tricks on me.

I watched Sweet Tooth eat a few things, including a meat pie (which it stole from some poor kid), a bucket of chips, half a doughnut and an ice cream (which it stole from the same poor kid). Every time Sweet Tooth went to eat something, it did the same thing, nodding as if to signal the meal was good to eat. Then it would just barge in and grab the food. By the end of lunch, it really did seem quite large.

'Okay, time to go, kids,' said Dad after we'd all had a swim. 'Time to head back home.'

We walked to the car, and Jaz and I got the sand out of the shoes, Mum got the sand out of the towels and Dad got the sand out of Mitch's mouth. It was then that I noticed Sweet Tooth had followed us to the car.

'Look, Jaz,' I joked. 'Sweet Tooth Seagull wants to come home with us.'

'Maybe it wants you to throw some more food,' she shrugged.

Sweet Tooth just stood near our car, watching us carefully. Its beady, black eyes darted around as though it was searching for something. It was like it was trying to work something out.

'Okay, that's freaky now,' said Jaz.

'Awww, it's just a seagull,' I replied quietly. 'Just an ordinary, harmless seagull.' Though something inside me suggested otherwise. It *was* a bit freaky. The way it watched us get into the car and drive off gave me goosebumps. It was like it was thinking. Thinking about *us*.

The drive back home was a long one. Dad put some music on to help him concentrate, and Mum read a book. Jaz and I played games on our smartphones, and Mitch picked the sand out of his shorts and ate it.

About an hour into the drive, I looked up from my game and saw something that sent a shiver down my spine. Just outside the window, flying next to our car, was Sweet Tooth! It flapped hard to stay near the car but was somehow keeping pace. Its sharp eyes were watching me through the window as it flew. My heart sped up and I looked back down at my game, not daring to look up again. This was becoming really weird. Really freaky. I decided that perhaps seagulls were not the nicest animals, after all.

THREE

It was almost dark when we finally got home, and everybody had to help unpack. Mum and Dad carried the suitcases in, and Jaz and I carried the board games and balls. Mitch didn't carry anything because he was too busy chasing a lizard with a stick. The lizard didn't have the stick, by the way. Mitch did. He was trying to swat the lizard with it. Poor lizard.

I didn't see Sweet Tooth as we unpacked, but I

could feel it watching us. I could feel it watching me. I was getting nervous, but I didn't say anything to anyone. I mean, what would I say, anyway? Hey, Jaz, that bird followed us 329 kilometres home from the beach. Hey, Mum, there's a weirdo seagull hiding in the trees. Hey, Dad, make sure you lock all the doors and windows because a strange bird is stalking me!

No, it was best not to say anything. I would just keep an eye out for it the next day. And if need be, I could feed it more ice cream or a salad roll to make it happy. Yes, that was it. It probably just wanted more food and it knew I liked feeding seagulls. That's what I would do – I would give it some more food. Then it would go away and leave me alone. Simple.

Later that night, I waited until everybody was asleep and then made my move. I had to be super sneaky to get past Mum and Dad's room. Luckily, Mum was snoring loudly and Dad was muttering something about the football (which he always did

when he slept). I tiptoed softly to the freezer and peered inside. Like always, there was lots of ice cream to choose from. Mitch had probably convinced Mum to buy more the last time they went shopping together. I took out a tub of strawberry. Perfect.

Armed with nothing but a spoon and half a tub of pink ice cream, I stepped outside. It was eerily quiet in our backyard. I made my way out to the middle of the lawn. The only sound was the gentle rustling of leaves high above. Could Sweet Tooth be up there? Was it watching me?

I heard a noise. What was it? Was it a flutter? Flapping feathers? I quickly turned around to where the noise had come from, but there were only shadows. I was scared. I mean, really scared.

Another noise, this time closer! I shivered and dropped the tub of ice cream. I'm a fairly brave girl, but that was it for me. I dashed inside and closed the door as quickly as I could. I ran to my bedroom and dived under the sheets! And that's where I stayed until morning.

As soon as the sun was up, I went straight to the backyard. Lying in the middle of the lawn, completely empty and spotless, was the ice-cream tub. Its contents had been eaten! I remembered the shadows and flapping noises from the night before. Sweet Tooth must have cleaned out the tub. I looked up at the trees for a sign of the bird. Nothing. The branches were empty. Perhaps my plan had worked and Sweet Tooth had gone back to the beach in search of its next meal. If so, I had done my job and the world was back to normal.

I could hear Dad yelling at Mitch back inside. Yep, the world was back to normal.

At breakfast, Dad said something exciting. 'Kids, we would like to take you to the movies today. I don't have to go back to work until Monday, so your mother and I thought we could do something fun as a family. One last holiday treat!'

I pumped my fist. 'Yes!'

Jaz pumped her fist. 'Yes!'

Mitch pumped his fist the wrong way and accidentally punched Dad on the chin. Silly Mitch.

Seeing a movie was great news. A beach holiday, now followed by a family trip to the flicks. I loved summer, and life was good. Mum and Dad were spoiling us with cool stuff, and Sweet Tooth was gone. It was the best I had felt in ages. Until we came home from the movies, that was.

FOUR

'I think we've been robbed!' gasped Mum as she opened the front door.

The house was a crazy mess. It looked like a giant bomb had hit it. The furniture was out of place, chairs had been upturned, magazines lay scattered across the floor, the curtains were torn and Mitch's secret sand collection had been knocked over. Honestly, who keeps a secret sand collection in their nappy drawer? Silly Mitch.

'Call the police!' sobbed Mum.

'Wait a minute,' said Dad, who always remained calm in situations like this. 'I don't think anything is actually missing.'

Dad had a point. The house was a pigsty, but whoever had broken in didn't seem to have taken anything.

I looked down and that's when I noticed the feather. An enormous, white plume lay on the living room floor among the mess. The size of the

feather worried me. Sweet Tooth was growing. I was about to pick it up when Mum screamed again. 'We *have* been robbed!'

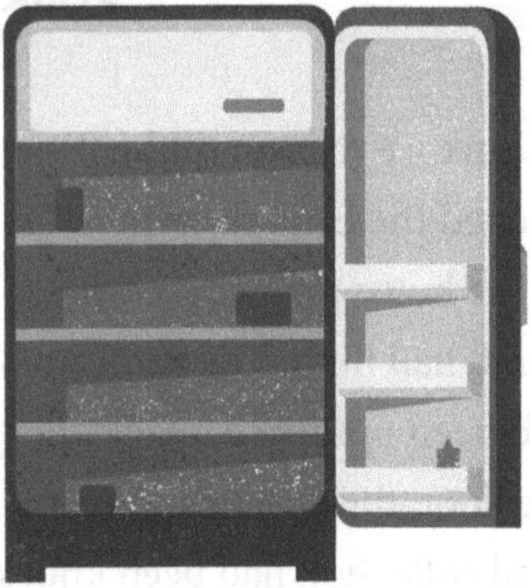

Mum was standing next to the fridge – a fridge that had been emptied of its contents. There was nothing left inside but empty jars and plastic containers. There was no questioning it now. Sweet Tooth had come into the house and eaten our food. I quickly picked up the feather and shoved it in my pocket. I had to keep this a secret. After all, it was me who'd fed the weirdo bird in the first place.

Dad locked all the doors and windows that night. The policeman who came to visit told him it would be a good idea to keep everything locked until the robber was caught. He also said that Dad should keep his pet birds in cages because he found some bird poo on the floor. Dad thought that was weird because we don't have any pet birds. Plus, the only thing that poos on the floor is Mitch. But I knew what had happened. I knew who had broken in.

I kept hearing noises outside my window that night. It was hard to sleep. Every now and then I heard a deep gush of wind and the flapping of giant feathers outside. I was glad Dad had locked everything. At one stage, a large shadow swept past my bedroom window. Sweet Tooth was clearly getting bigger, and it scared me to imagine what it would need to eat next. I decided to turn on my radio to distract myself.

'We interrupt this programme for breaking news,' said a man on the radio. 'There have been several robberies in the local area this evening, and residents are warned to keep their homes locked up.'

I sat up in bed and listened closely.

'The early reports are that the thief is trashing

homes in search of food. One lady claims that a giant seagull trapped her in the bathroom while it cleaned out her whole fridge and attacked her husband! She is being questioned by police for further information'.

I switched the radio off and thought hard. What was happening? What had I started? Sweet Tooth was turning into a monster and something had to be done. The hungry bird was attacking people! I had to stop it before it hurt somebody. Or, even worse – ate somebody!

I made a plan and put my head back down on the pillow. The plan was risky, but maybe, just maybe, it would work.

FIVE

The next day was a day I'll never forget. When I woke up, everybody was watching the television.

'Look at this, Lara!' yelled Jaz when she saw me. 'That bird is on TV!'

Sure enough, right there on the morning news, was Sweet Tooth. The dark spots on its chest could only belong to one bird. There was blurry footage of it knocking over bins at the shopping centre. The bins looked tiny compared to Sweet Tooth. I gulped.

'What's it doing?' I asked, suddenly feeling sick in the stomach.

'It's terrorising the whole community, that's what!' gasped Dad. 'It's destroyed several houses and is currently eating all the food in the supermarket. Nobody knows what to do because it's so big. It's as big as a bus! They say it is even eating people!'

'The whole town is in lockdown!' shrieked Mum (who only shrieked when she was really freaked out). 'Nobody is allowed to leave their home!'

'You kids are to stay right here with us,' said Dad, looking serious. 'You can't leave my sight until the situation is safe. Nobody is to leave this house.'

That wasn't good news for me because part of my plan involved leaving the house. Thankfully, I had already thought about this and had worked out a way to get around it.

'Dad, it's probably not a good time to tell you this,' I said. 'But Jaz painted your study desk purple.'

'Did not!' argued a surprised Jaz. 'Mitch did it!'

'What have you done?' yelled Dad, grabbing Mitch by the arm and storming down the hallway. Mum and Jaz followed close behind. They had forgotten about the TV and wanted to find out what was going on in the study.

The start of my plan had worked, and it was time to act. I quickly dashed to Mitch's room and looked under his bed. Sure enough, his secret ice-cream stash was there. Honestly, who keeps a secret ice-cream stash under their bed? I grabbed the closest container of melted dairy and ran to the front door. I could hear lots of yelling in the study. I hurried outside, picked up my bike and rode down the side of our house to the street. I was scared but I knew what

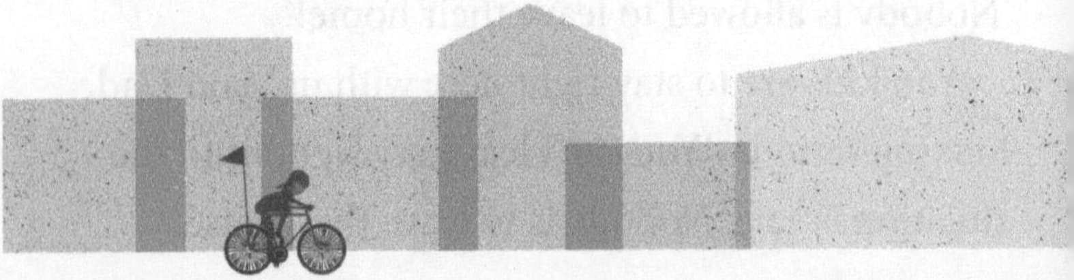

I had to do. As I pedalled down the road, I could hear Mum and Dad screaming at Mitch. Silly Mitch. (I never did tell him the truth about that desk.)

I rode straight for the centre of town. Sweet Tooth was there, and the ice cream under my arm would fix this whole nightmare.

I could hear a commotion as I approached town. There was lots of crashing, banging, shouting, thumping, squawking and clanging – all that noise and I couldn't even see anybody – or anything. The streets were empty.

I knew where the noise was coming from as I got closer to the main street. The chaos was coming from the supermarket. Sweet Tooth was still there. I rode my bike through the empty car park and put it down outside the main doors.

'It's too big!' yelled a voice from somewhere inside the shop. 'Quick, run for your lives!'

The doors of the supermarket suddenly burst

open, and two firefighters dashed past me. They were closely followed by the supermarket manager and a tubby policeman. 'Get out of here, little girl!' puffed the large officer as he waddled by. 'That bird just ate someone!'

The fleeing men disappeared in seconds, and I was soon left alone outside the supermarket. I heard an angry squawk come from inside. This was followed by silence. The only noise I could hear was the hum of a news helicopter high in the sky. And that's when I did it. Tucking the melted ice cream under my arm, I pushed the doors open and stepped inside.

SIX

Sweet Tooth was enormous. Massive. Huge. Chunky, chunky fatso. It was the biggest animal I had ever seen. It was about ten times bigger than the elephant I saw at the zoo. I began to wonder what I was even doing there, alone with a devil bird. This was no place for a girl.

Sweet Tooth's feathered body filled most of the shop. Empty food shelves lay scattered around the ghastly gull and, luckily for me, it was looking the other way, otherwise it may have eaten me then and there. It had its back to me and was busily demolishing the bread section, sucking whole loaves through its beak as if they were tiny crumbs.

I decided my plan was too risky and I started walking backwards towards the door. And that's when I did it – I accidentally bumped into a trolley, sending it crashing into the wall. Sweet Tooth spun around and looked at me with its hungry eyes. It looked at the ice cream under my arm and nodded slowly. That was the signal, and I knew I could only do one thing – run!

I left that supermarket faster than Jaz could say 'Mitch did it', and picked up my bike. Behind me, I heard a deep cracking sound and turned to see the roof of the supermarket beginning to shake. I jumped onto my bike and pedalled as fast as I could. I turned around again to see Sweet Tooth's head smash through the roof, sending tiles and bits of wood in all directions. I ducked as a plank of wood smashed on the concrete next to where I rode. I didn't look back again, but from the crashing noises I knew that Sweet Tooth had some work to do before it could escape.

I must have pedalled for about a minute when I heard an explosion behind me and the flapping of enormous feathers. Sweet Tooth was loose. A gush

of wind swept me over and I came tumbling off my bike, landing on the side of the road, the ice cream still tucked under my arm. The ground shook and I looked up to see Sweet Tooth land in the middle of the road. Its wings were so big that they knocked over the chimneys of the surrounding houses.

I slowly stood up and faced the beast.

'Go away!' I yelled at the top of my voice. 'Just leave us all alone!'

The bird just looked at me, blinking in the sunlight. Its crazed eyes zeroed in on the ice cream under my arm.

'Keep the bird there!' yelled an unfamiliar voice

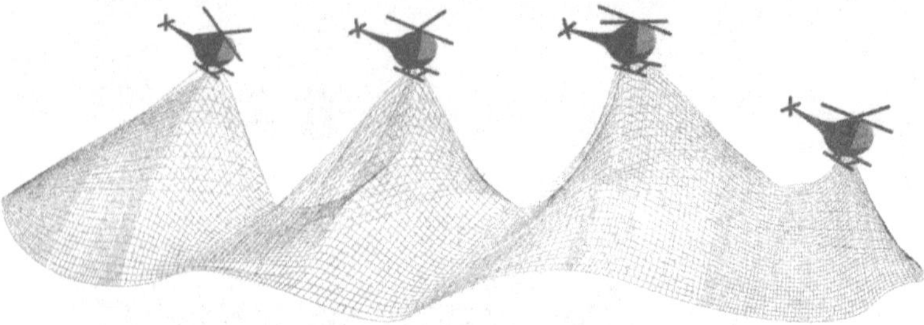

from above. I looked up and saw four helicopters flying over Sweet Tooth. 'Do your best to keep the bird there!' said the voice again. One of the pilots was shouting through a microphone.

It's a good thing seagulls don't know English, otherwise there would have been trouble. Mind you, Mitch doesn't know English and there's always trouble with him.

Sweet Tooth suddenly lurched at the ice cream under my arm, but I managed to duck out of the way just in time. I took a few steps backwards, taking the lid off the ice cream. It was completely melted, having spent most of its life under Mitch's bed, and some dripped from the lid onto the road. Sweet Tooth lunged towards my feet, and I jumped back as it sucked the ice cream from the street.

I took a few more steps backwards and deliberately tipped more ice cream onto the road. Sweet Tooth jerked its giant neck forward and sucked up the sticky mess almost as quickly as it hit the tar. I did the same thing again, tipping ice cream onto the pavement. Sweet Tooth lunged and sucked it up with lightning speed. I stepped back and did the same thing, over and over again. For about two minutes I crept backwards, tipping bits of ice cream onto the road. Then something terrible happened. I ran out of ice cream.

'Uh-oh,' I said, looking into the empty container. I was trapped now. What would Sweet Tooth eat next? Me?

Without thinking, I threw the empty tub at the bird, but it snapped it up in one gulp!

I stood empty-handed, face-to-face with the weirdest, hungriest bird on the planet. Sweet Tooth took one look at me and then puffed out its spotted chest. It nodded slowly. I screamed and curled into a ball, waiting to be swallowed alive.

Instead of hearing the snapping of a giant beak, I heard a loud whoosh in the sky above. I looked up to see a giant net fall from between the four helicopters that had been waiting above. Sweet Tooth tried to flap its wings to break free from the gigantic trap, but

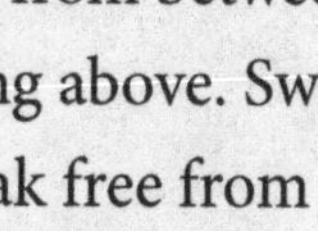

the more it struggled, the more it became caught in the net.

'Well done, kiddo,' said the pilot into his microphone. 'You did good.'

It took a long time for things to settle down after that day. I must have done about a hundred interviews for the television and radio shows – everybody wanted to hear the story of the bravest girl in the world, the girl who'd stood in danger's way to help catch a monster. Eventually, the reporters stopped knocking on our door.

I told them all the same thing, though, that it was my brother Mitch who was the real hero. It was his craving for ice cream

that had kept our house full of the stuff. If it wasn't for him, there wouldn't have been a stash under the bed. I would have had nothing to keep the giant seagull distracted while the helicopters steadied their net. Mitch was the hero. Mitch and his ice cream.

As for the giant man-eating, ice-cream-loving gull, it got taken to the city zoo. They built an enormous aviary just for Sweet Tooth. Lots of tourists come to look at it. They fly from all over the country to get a look at the world's largest bird.

We went to visit the zoo yesterday. Thousands of people were there, all to see Sweet Tooth, of course. I don't think the zoo is very smart, though, because they have just begun building a new ice-cream stand right next to Sweet Tooth's cage. Silly zoo.

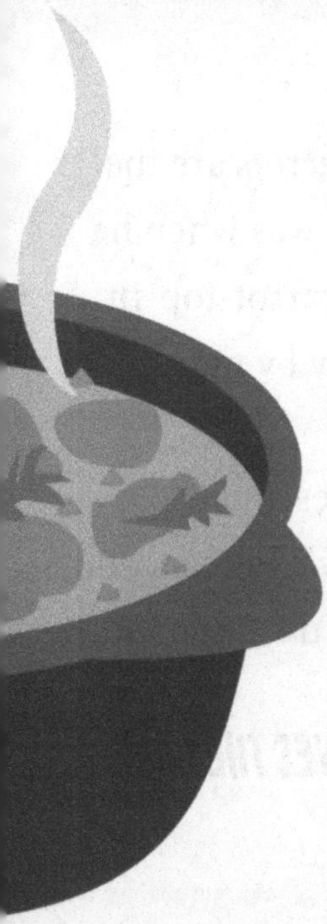

TANGENT CHICKEN SOUP

Prep Time: 15 minutes
Cook Time: 60 minutes

INGREDIENTS:

1. *4 chicken thigh cutlets.* Chicken cutlets… cutlets. My mum used to make lamb cutlets. They were really nice because I'd dollop extra barbecue sauce over them. Dad thought the amount of sauce I put on the lamb cutlets was ridiculous, but I knew what I was doing. Barbecue sauce has special powers and makes anything else taste better. I didn't like yoghurt until I mixed barbecue sauce in with it. Delicious! De. Li. Cious.

(2) *2 large carrots, finely chopped.* Carrots are the same colour as my brother's hair was when he was little. He used to get called 'carrot-top' in the playground at school. Usually by me.

(3) *1 large onion, finely chopped.* Does 'finely' mean 'really small' or 'excellently'? I mean, you could chop an onion in half and do a fine job.

WHAT FINELY CHOPPED ONION HALVES THEY ARE, YOUNG MAN.

I think I did a fine job with these halves, too. Thank you very much.

YOU'RE QUITE WELCOME.

Who is this I am talking to?

NOBODY.

Oh, okay. Well, I'd better get back to the recipe then.

(4) *2 garlic cloves, finely chopped.* There's that word again. Finely. Does that mean that, if somebody says to you, 'You're looking fine today, young man', that you are looking really skinny like a finely chopped onion? That could be quite an insult if you were trying to become the prop-forward in your footy team. I like footy. I go for the Parramatta Eels.

I'M AN AFL GIRL. I GO FOR THE RICHMOND TIGERS.

Ahh… so you're a girl.

NO I'M NOT. I DIDN'T SAY ANYTHING.

Yes you did! You said, 'I'm an AFL girl'.

NO I DIDN'T.

Who are you? And why do you keep interrupting my recipe?

NOBODY.

Whatever. I'd better get back to the ingredients.

5 *1 thin celery stick, chopped into skinny little pieces.*

6 *¼ cup of parsley, chopped in an excellent manner,* worthy of praise, leading to commendation.

7 *8 cups of water.* I think this has to be one of the most boring ingredients that I have ever seen in a recipe. Water. You may as well just say 'air'. Recipes are supposed to be interesting, not boring.

I THINK YOU'VE MISSED THE POINT, YOUNG MAN.

You again! Who are you?

SOMEBODY WHO KNOWS MORE ABOUT COOKING THAN YOU. THE WATER WILL SOAK UP THE FLAVOURS OF THE OTHER INGREDIENTS. IT IS ALSO THE LIQUIDITY THAT MAKES SOUP, SOUP.

Oh, I didn't know that.

YOU LEARN SOMETHING NEW EVERY DAY.

I'd like to learn who you are. Please just tell me.

I'M NOT TELLING YOU WHO I AM.

Well, I know that you're a girl, you go for the Richmond Tigers and you know a thing or two about cooking.

I'M STILL NOT TELLING.

You're annoying me by not telling. Anyway, let me get back on track. Stop creating tangents.

8 *½ teaspoon of pepper.* I wonder why pepper makes you sneeze. The police in America use pepper spray to subdue dangerous criminals, but the criminals scream instead of sneeze. The Beatles wrote 'Sgt Pepper's Lonely Hearts Club Band'. Was he lonely because he kept sneezing?

(9) *½ teaspoon of salt.* Salt and vinegar chips are the best. One time, my best friend and I ate such a strong batch of salt and vinegar chips that we actually sweated. But we call sweated 'swat' because it sounds like past tense.

AND YOU THINK THE AMERICANS ARE WEIRD.

Argh! Stop interrupting.

BUT I THOUGHT YOU WANTED TO FIND OUT WHO I WAS.

I do. Please tell me.

NO.

Then why are you interrupting again?

BECAUSE YOU'RE A WEIRDO.

Why?

WHO CALLS SWEATED 'SWAT'? THAT'S PLAIN LOOPY. AND YOU THINK AMERICANS ARE STRANGE.

Just forget it. I need to get to the cooking steps. That's enough tangents for one recipe.

STEPS:

1. Walk to the cupboard.
2. Look at the desired cupboard door.
3. Reach out with your hand.
4. Open the cupboard door.
5. Reach in with your hand.
6. Grab a saucepan by the handle.
7. Pull the saucepan out of the cupboard.
8. Close the cupboard door.

9. Walk over to the sink with the saucepan still in your hand.
10. Place the saucepan under the tap.
11. Reach out with your other hand.
12. Turn the tap on.
13. Watch the water come out.
14. Half-fill the saucepan with water.
15. Turn the tap off.
16. Blink.
17. Carry the saucepan over to the cooktop.
18. Place the saucepan onto the desired hot plate.
19. Turn on the hot plate.
20. Blink again.

ARE YOU SERIOUSLY GOING TO GO THROUGH EVERY STEP IN SUCH FINE DETAIL?

Thank you very much. I'm glad you think I'm doing an excellent job.

NOT THAT 'FINE', YOU DRONGO.

Oh.

PEOPLE DON'T NEED TO KNOW EVERY SINGLE DETAIL, YOU KNOW. THEY CAN WORK A LOT OUT FOR THEMSELVES.

So, I don't need to describe every step?

OF COURSE NOT!

That's actually quite useful information. Thanks.

YOU'RE WELCOME, TIM.

Woah! You know my name!

DANG IT.

Aha. Now I have another clue. So far, I know that you're a girl, you go for the Richmond Tigers, you know a thing or two about cooking and you know my name!

IT WAS A LUCKY GUESS.

I don't believe you. Anyway, back to instruction land.

21 Combine the carrots, onion, garlic, celery, parsley, pepper and salt in the water. Simmer on a low heat for about 15 minutes.

LOOK, SORRY TO INTERRUPT AGAIN, BUT THAT SOUNDS WEIRD.

What sounds weird?

PEPPER AND SALT. IT SHOULD BE SALT AND PEPPER.

It doesn't have to be.

BUT IT SHOULD BE. EVERYONE SAYS 'SALT AND PEPPER'.

Not everyone does. Plus, that's the order they appeared in the ingredients section.

IT DOESN'T MATTER. MOST PEOPLE CALL IT 'SALT AND PEPPER'. MOST NORMAL PEOPLE, ANYWAY.

I'm normal.

NO YOU'RE NOT. YOU SAY WEIRD THINGS AND YOU WRITE WEIRD BOOKS.

I don't mean to be rude, but I think you're a grammar freak.

I'M KNOWN TO BE.

Is that another clue?

YES... YES... THAT WAS ANOTHER CLUE.

Okay, so you're a girl, you go for the Richmond Tigers, you know a thing or two about cooking, you know my name and you're a grammar freak.

SOMETHING LIKE THAT.

Hmmmm… well, I'll keep thinking. But in the meantime, back to the steps.

22 Cut the chicken off the bone. Use a fork to strip the chicken into stringy pieces. Add to the soup and allow to simmer for 45 minutes.

23 Serve with any leftover parsley.

24 Now that I don't have to describe every step in detail, this is really quite easy. Though, sometimes, easy things aren't as easy as they seem. One time, I went shopping for new pants with my mum. I had to try them on in the changing room. Which is easy enough, except what I thought was the changing room turned out to be the lift. The lift doors were the same colour as the changing room doors. How was I supposed to know? I had stripped off my old pants and was about to put the

new pants on when the doors opened at the women's underwear level.

WOAH, WOAH, WOAH! SPARE ME THE DETAILS! YOU'RE SUPPOSED TO BE GOING THROUGH THE CHICKEN SOUP RECIPE.

I am.

NO YOU'RE NOT. YOU'RE GOING OFF TRACK. YOU'RE ON ANOTHER TANGENT.

You can't talk. You've been jumping in and putting me off track more than anything!

I HAVE A SHORT ATTENTION SPAN. IT'S WHAT I DO.

You're a strange girl. But in a funny way, I find you likeable.

YOU SHOULD PROBABLY GET BACK TO YOUR CHANGING ROOM LIFT STORY.

But you said I should get back on track.

IT'S AN INTERESTING STORY. I WANT TO HEAR HOW IT TURNS OUT.

So, there I am, stripped down to my underpants when the lift doors open to the women's underwear section. Which is fair enough, because I got confused with the rooms, but unfortunately my underpants got stuck to my old pants when I pulled them off. I was naked.

WHAT! YOU WERE NAKED WHEN THE DOORS OPENED?

Yep.

WHAT DID ALL THOSE WOMEN DO?

I can't remember because I fainted. But when I woke up I was drenched. I swat badly under the stress.

LOL. WOBBLY WOULD LOVE THAT STORY.

Who's Wobbly?

MY BEST FRIEND.

Another clue!

THE FINAL CLUE.

The final clue?

YES. I'M NOT GOING TO GIVE YOU ANY MORE CLUES BECAUSE THE NEXT STEP IS THE FINAL STEP IN THE RECIPE.

How do you know it's going to be the final step?

BECAUSE I KNOW A THING OR TWO ABOUT COOKING, REMEMBER?

Oh yeah. Well, that leaves me with six clues. You're a girl, you go for the Richmond Tigers, you know a thing or two about cooking, you know my name, you're a grammar freak and your best friend is Wobbly.

THAT'S ME!

But who are you??

A NEW CHARACTER.

A new character?

FOR A STORY LATER IN THIS BOOK.

Really?

YES INDEED. I'VE GIVEN YOU ENOUGH INFORMATION ABOUT MYSELF, AND NOW YOU CAN WRITE A STORY ABOUT ME!

Do I have to?

YES. ABSOLUTELY!

And if I do, will you stop interrupting my recipes?

I'LL TRY. BUT I CAN'T PROMISE ANYTHING. THEY DON'T CALL ME TANGENTINE FOR NOTHING.

Is that your name?

ARGH! AARRGGHH!!

Ha! I know your name! You're Tangentine!

OKAY, OKAY... LOOK, I'D BETTER GET GOING. I'VE GIVEN YOU ENOUGH TO GET ON WITH. I EXPECT MY STORY TO BE A GOOD ONE. MAKE IT INTERESTING. MAKE IT ABOUT ORDERING PIZZA OVER THE PHONE.

I prefer ordering pizza online.

I KNOW YOU DO. BUT THAT'S NOT THE POINT. I WANT MY STORY TO BE ABOUT ORDERING IT OVER THE PHONE. NOW, YOU GO AND GET CRACKING ON MY STORY. MAKE SURE IT'S GOOD!

I'll try.

AND ALL THE BEST WITH THE FINAL STEP OF THE SOUP RECIPE.

Thanks. Oh, that reminds me…

25 Enjoy!

DOCTOR GENRE

PART ONE

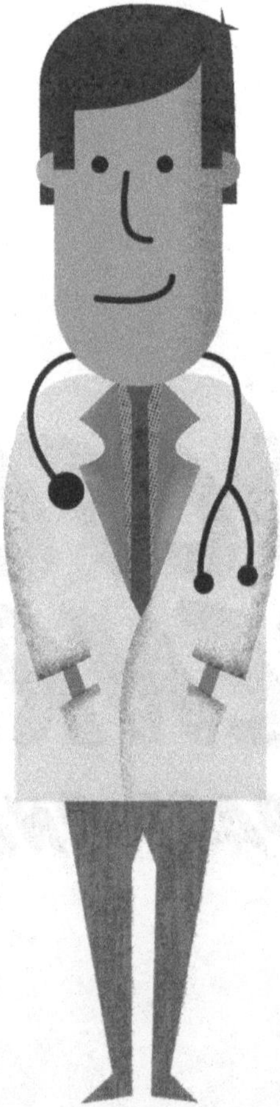

DOCTOR NORMAL

Jimmy wiped his nose with a tissue and blinked miserably at his mother. The doctor's waiting room was almost empty, and his appointment was next.

Jimmy coughed into his sleeve, then rubbed his sore throat.

'There, there,' smiled his mother, giving him a reassuring look. 'It will be okay. It's just a cold, honey.'

'Jimmy Jenkins,' announced Doctor Normal, opening the door to his normal office.

Jimmy stood up and followed Doctor Normal into his normal office. It smelled like hygiene, and there was the usual doctor's picture of a human body on the wall.

'What seems to be the problem, young man?' asked Doctor Normal.

'I have a runny nose, sore throat, blocked ears, headache and fever,' said Jimmy.

Doctor Normal scribbled something down on his normal doctor's notepad. 'It appears you have a normal cold,' he said.

Jimmy nodded. It was just as he'd expected.

Doctor Normal handed him a prescription, then showed him to the door.

DOCTOR HORROR

Jimmy wiped his bloodied nose with a tissue and looked helplessly at his mother. The doctor's waiting room was eerily empty, and his appointment was next.

Jimmy coughed more blood into his sleeve, then ran a finger along his throat, signalling the fate that awaited him.

'Now, now,' managed his mother, wrapping her arms around him. 'I have a baaaad feeling about this.'

'JIMMY JENKINS,' roared Doctor Horror, smashing through the door of his office.

Doctor Horror grabbed Jimmy by the arm and dragged him into his dark office. It smelled of centuries-old dust, and there was a cluster of black bats hanging from the ceiling in one corner.

'I would be most keen to sample your blood,' said Doctor Horror, reaching for his favourite needle.

'Er, I only have a cold,' replied Jimmy.

But it was too late. Doctor Horror had drained a sample and was already adding it to a large collection of blood-filled vials in his cupboard.

Jimmy was so horrified, he screamed and crashed right back through the door!

DOCTOR PLAY SCHOOL

Jimmy pretended to wipe his nose with a tissue and blinked happily at the television camera. The studio lights were on and filming had begun.

Jimmy faked a gentle cough and smiled at the camera.

'There, there,' smiled his actor mother, stepping on-screen. She, too, looked at the camera. 'Have you ever had a nasty cold? Sometimes, little boys and girls get sick. That means it's time to visit the doctor.'

'Jimmy Jenkins,' grinned Doctor Play School, joining the others on camera.

Jimmy shook Doctor Play School's hand and stepped into the Play School office. It smelled like playthings, and there was a picture of Big Ted on the wall.

'What seems to be the problem, young man?' said Doctor Play School.

'I have a little tickle in my throat,' said Jimmy.

Doctor Play School smiled and looked at the camera. 'I know a song about throat tickles,' he said.

Jimmy coughed in time with the music, and listened as Doctor Play School sang his throat-tickle song.

Doctor Play School handed Little Ted and a cup of red cordial to Jimmy, then showed him to the door.

DOCTOR COMEDY

Jimmy wiped his nose with a tissue and farted at his mother. The doctor's waiting room was almost empty, which was a shame, because he would have enjoyed watching other people smell that beauty.

Jimmy burped into his sleeve, then pulled a ridiculous face at the man sitting opposite.

'Teehee,' giggled his mother. 'You are one big, fat crack-up!'

'Jimmy Jenkins,' yodelled Doctor Comedy, stepping from behind his door, dressed in a clown outfit.

Jimmy stood up and followed Doctor Comedy into the office, but Doctor Comedy turned around and tickled Jimmy, which sent Jimmy into a fit of laughter. The office smelled like sunshine, and there was a picture of Adam Sandler on the wall.

'What seems to be the prob, Bob?' asked Doctor Comedy.

'I have a runny nose, sore throat, blocked ears, headache and fever,' said Jimmy.

Doctor Comedy stared at Jimmy for a moment before bursting out laughing. 'That's a good one,' he said.

Jimmy grinned and pulled a silly face.

Doctor Comedy took turns pulling silly faces with Jimmy, then showed him to the door.

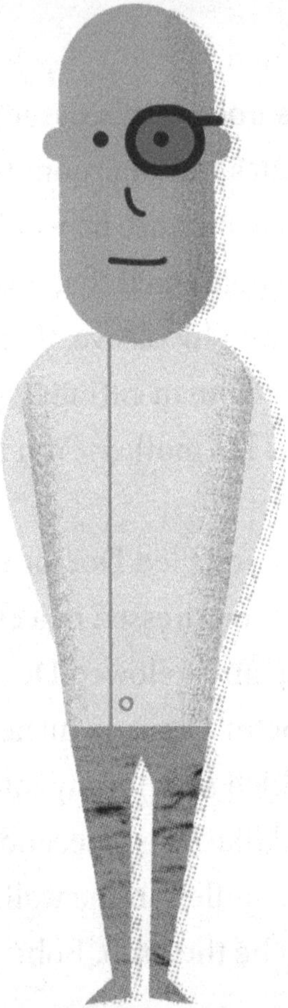

DOCTOR SCI-FI

Jimmy wiped his nose with a tissue and blinked miserably at his mother. The virtual waiting room was almost empty, and his hologram-transmission appointment was next.

Jimmy coughed into his sleeve, then rubbed his sore throat.

'There, there,' smiled his mother, giving him a reassuring look. 'You'll be cured in about 34 seconds from now.'

'Jimmy Jenkins,' announced Doctor Sci-Fi, appearing in hologram-transmission form in front of Jimmy and his mother.

Jimmy stood up out of politeness, then sat back down on his magnetic-glider chair. He changed the poster on his bedroom wall via thought control to one of his favourite robot bands.

'What seems to be the problem, young man?' asked Doctor Sci-Fi.

'I have a runny nose, sore throat, blocked ears, headache and fever,' said Jimmy.

Doctor Sci-Fi pointed to an electro-health pad, which had formed itself on Jimmy's operating system. 'Code 1-5-6-H required,' said Doctor Sci-Fi.

Jimmy placed his index finger on the electro-health pad, and Doctor Sci-Fi looked at the readings.

Doctor Sci-Fi sent a tiny rejuvenation capsule via light-speed drone to Jimmy, who swallowed it at once.

Jimmy smiled. He was healed.

Doctor Sci-Fi saved the digital readings, then showed him how to use a door to access other worlds.

ONE

I used to like shopping. As a toddler, I would sit high in the trolley while Mum pushed me past rows and rows of shiny products. I would sit there nicely – being a good boy – pretending to do the right thing. But really I was waiting. Waiting for the right time to strike. Waiting for the right time to ambush. I knew what was coming. Mum knew what was coming. It was just a matter of time. And when the trolley finally made its slow turn into my favourite aisle, I would prepare myself for the act.

'Mummy! Chocky yum-yums!' I would squeal in my cutest toddler voice.

'Not today, Noah. Mummy needs to keep walking,' she would say.

'Ooooh! Lolly yum-yums!' I would giggle, pointing to the packets of jelly beans.

'No, Noah. Maybe another time,' she would reply, looking uneasily at the other shoppers.

'Mmmmm! Chippie chip-chips!'

She'd ignore me.

'Yum-yum gummy bears!'

She'd shake her head, trying not to look at me.

It was at this point, usually about halfway down the colourful corridor of confectionery, that I would put on my Hollywood best.

'Polly-lops! Polly-lops!' My voice would rise with urgency and excitement.

Mum would shake her head again, though more nervously.

'Pwease, Mummy?' The tone of my voice would soften as my bottom lip would start to tremble. 'Pwitty, pwitty pwease.'

I would look desperately at Mum. She would look back at me with fearful eyes. We both knew what was coming. I would take a deep breath in preparation for my Oscar nomination.

'I WANT LOLLY!' I would shout. The supermarket music faded beneath my shrill cries.

'LOLLY, LOLLY, LOLLY!' I would chant, clenching my fists as I banged the edge of the trolley. It was at this point that the other customers would start to stare at us.

Once, a rather tubby lady stood right next to me when I exploded.

'GUMMY, GUMMY, GUMMY!' I shouted, beating my chest like a wild ape.

'What a rude little boy,' said the large lady.

'FAT, FAT, FATTY!' I screeched back at her.

She gasped and dropped the chocolate bar she had just taken off the shelf.

Mum was furious. 'Noah! You're putting on a show! Stop it at once!'

'I WANT LOLLIES! I WANT LOLLIES!'

It was about this time that the supermarket staff began to approach us, and Mum gave in.

'Sshh! Okay, here – have this!' she'd snapped, shoving a candy bar into my demanding little hands.

Yes, I used to like shopping. The thought of a tasty reward for my silver-screen performances made the trips worthwhile. Lollypops were a bare minimum. I would often score packets of chewy chocolate bars and bags of sticky sweets.

Being the town's most talented tantrum toddler was great, but everything changed when I started going to school. Mum went back to work, and our shopping trips were done on the weekends with Dad there, too. There was no use even trying to put on an act in front of him. He was too strict. Shopping started to become boring and I began to hate each new trip more than the last. I had to trudge quietly behind the trolley as Mum and Dad ticked off their lists and checked the prices. By the time I reached

Year Four, shopping was officially private enemy number one. It was my pet hate.

TWO

The 12th of May is a date I'll never forget. On 12 May last year, it rained so hard that my football game was cancelled.

'Don't worry, Noah,' said Dad, patting me on the back. 'There's always next week.'

I loved playing football, and it was disappointing to have the game called off. What was more disappointing was what Dad said next.

'There are a few things your mother and I need to pick up from the shops today, so we're going there instead.'

'Awww,' I moaned. I couldn't stand the thought of shopping at the best of times.

'Get dressed,' said Dad firmly. 'We leave in five.'

'Can't I stay here and play Quarrycraft?' I protested. 'I'm almost up to the level with the gemstone jet.'

Quarrycraft was my favourite computer game.

'No, Noah. Go and get dressed.'

'I am dressed,' I replied.

'Underpants and a hat don't count,' he sighed.

I went back to my room and closed the door, preparing to hold everything up as long as I could.

'Noah, hurry up!' called Mum a few minutes later. 'Your father is waiting in the car.'

'But I need to choose new undies!' I called back.

Mum wasn't happy. 'What about the ones you were wearing before?'

'They were too green!' I called back. 'I'm wearing yellow ones instead.'

'Don't be silly,' she groaned. 'Just get dressed!'

'Is it hot or cold today?' I asked, trying to buy more time.

'It's in-between,' she replied. 'Just wear whatever you feel like wearing.'

'So blue undies and a hat?'

'What happened to the yellow undies?' she demanded.

'They were too yellow.'

Mum groaned.

I grinned. I was only just warming up.

'So… is it on the hot side of cold or the cold side of hot?' I asked.

'It's raining, for goodness sake!' she yelled. 'Quickly pick something!'

'So a raincoat and umbrella?' I replied.

Mum was getting frustrated. 'The shops are inside! Now, hurry up, Noah!'

I was glad I didn't push the conversation further. When I got to the car, Dad's face was red and he glared at me. 'What took you so long?!'

'Mum told me to wear the wrong thing,' I lied.

Mum gave Dad one of those looks that mums

give dads, and he knew I was fibbing. 'I'm very disappointed in your behaviour this morning,' he said.

'I'm very disappointed we're going shopping,' I echoed, though not too loudly.

We drove in silence for a while before Mum said something that made things even worse. 'We're going to try out a new shopping centre today. It's the biggest shopping centre in the whole city, so we might be there for a while. It only opened last month.'

'What's it called?' I whined.

'Three Bag Mall. It has twelve levels of shops,' she replied. 'Don't worry, we'll have something nice for morning tea and lunch,' she added, trying to cheer me up.

'And dinner,' said Dad. 'It may take us all day to look at the shops.'

And that's how 12 May started. My football game was washed out and I had to go shopping. I had to spend the whole day doing what I hated more than anything else.

It was time to make a drama out of this. I may not have been a toddler any more, but Mum and Dad were going to see the biggest tantrum of their lives.

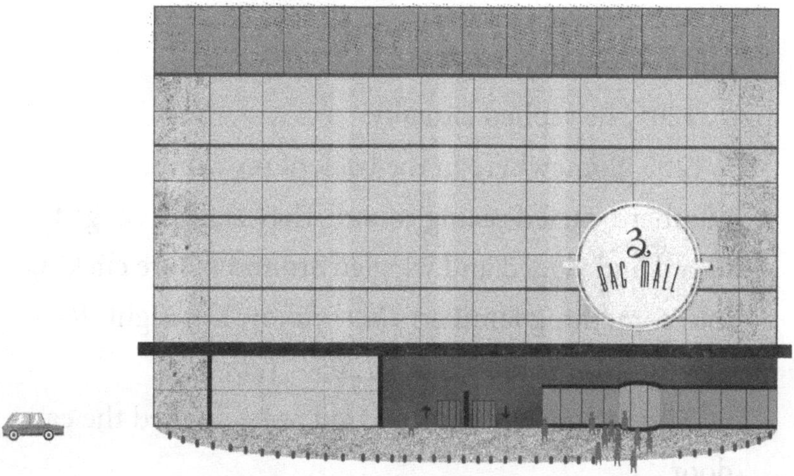

THREE

Our car pulled into the car park of Three Bag Mall. It was massive – easily the biggest car park I had ever seen.

'Wow,' said Mum, pointing to one of the busy shop entrances. 'This place is gigantic.'

'It's huge!' gasped Dad.

'It's enormous!' cried Mum.

'Titanic in torture power,' I said. And it was. All I could see was shops. Nothing but stores, stands and supermarkets. I was doomed. 'I should be back at home playing Quarrycraft,' I muttered to myself.

Before we got out of the car, Mum turned to Dad. 'Honey,' she said. 'What was the secret number for our new credit cards?'

'1205,' he replied casually.

1205. Somewhere in the back of my mind, numbers started racing round. They zigged, zagged, jigged and jagged and wiggled around before clicking into something familiar. *That's funny*, I thought. *It's the same as the date today. 1205 – 12th May.*

'Time to go!' announced Dad as he opened the car door.

'Time to shop,' said Mum.

Time to tantrum, I thought to myself.

We left the car and headed to the main entrance. The car-park noises disappeared and were replaced by the buzzing sounds of the centre. It was the most

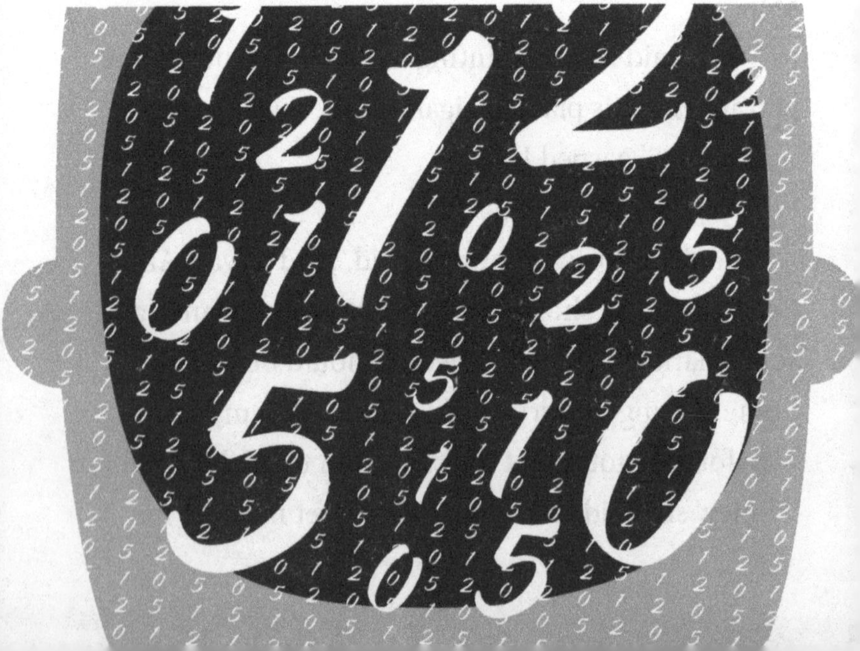

enormous mall I had ever seen – and we were only in the foyer! There were hundreds of shops going off in every direction. There were lifts, escalators and stairs that connected to the upper levels of the mall. I couldn't even see the top. I shivered at the thought of being there all day.

We went up a few levels to our first stop – the bank. Mum and Dad had to sort out something with their new credit cards. I had to sit quietly and pretend to have good manners while they talked to the bank manager.

'I understand you would like to increase the limit on your cards,' said the manager.

'That's right,' replied Dad.

I was so bored.

'Please complete this form,' smiled the manager, handing a piece of paper to Dad.

So, so bored.

'I have a question,' said Mum.

Great, I thought. *More tiresome talk*. My mind began to drift into planning mode. I had to get myself out of this mind-numbing situation.

'Your face is ugly!' I blurted, pointing to the manager.

'Excuse me?' he asked, looking shocked.

'You're excused,' I replied. 'No need to apologise for burps and farts.'

Dad gave me a grimacing glare. Mum looked horrified.

'I beg your pardon?' demanded the manager, looking both surprised and cranky.

'Burps and farts – no need to apologise,' I clarified.

Mum and Dad were too stunned to say or do anything. I don't think they could believe what I was saying. I don't think *I* could believe what I was saying. The bank manager couldn't believe it, either. 'Well… in my life… I never –'

'Of course you have!' I interrupted. 'We all do burps and farts.'

Dad snapped into gear and grabbed me by the ear. 'Outside now!' he choked, pulling me away from the meeting. He marched me outside and ordered me to sit on a chair. And that's where I stayed for the rest of the bank meeting. It cost me six months' pocket money, which was a shame, but at least I didn't have to listen to the boring conversation.

Mum and Dad were embarrassed by my behaviour – though, luckily for me, they were also hungry, and our next stop was morning tea. Mum wanted to try out a new Japanese cafe that had a good name.

'I can't believe how rude you were in the bank,' she sighed. 'Do you really hate shopping that much?'

'Yup,' I replied.

Dad pointed an angry finger at me. 'Noah, if you act like that again today, I am banning your pocket money for another six months, and you won't be able to play Quarrycraft, either.'

Silence.

Dad meant business. I gulped an uncertain gulp. I thought about it for a while. Six months plus six months was twelve months. That was a year. A year was a long time without pocket money and my favourite computer game. I decided tantrums were

probably not the best form of shopping self-defence after all. I had to find another way to get through this day from hell.

Just then, a Japanese waitress came over to take our order.

'I'll have some Japanese tea and a small donburi,' said Mum.

'Same for me,' said Dad.

'And for the boy?' asked the waitress, looking at me.

'Do you have fruit juice?' I asked.

'Hai,' she replied.

'Hello,' I said. 'Do you have fruit juice?'

'Hai,' she said again.

'Ummm… yes, hello. Do you have fruit juice?'

'Hai!' she repeated, annoyance creeping into her voice.

'HELLOOOO!' I sang back. 'DO YOU HAVE ANY

LIQUID JUICE THAT COMES FROM FRUIT?!'

'HAI, HAI, HAI! YES, YES, YES!' she howled back.

'No need to go off!' I staggered, surprised by her outburst. 'I'll have an apple juice, thanks.'

I looked at Mum and Dad for help. I couldn't work out what had just happened.

In between chuckles, Mum explained. 'Hai means yes in Japanese!' She must have forgotten about the bank, which was good because she was still smiling.

I would usually see the funny side of this, but not today. I was not in the mood. I detested shopping, and nothing was going to cheer me up. I sat and sulked for the rest of morning tea.

FOUR

After morning tea, we went back to doing the worst thing in the world – shopping. Mum and Dad decided to go separate ways. 'That way we can cover more ground,' said Dad.

'Good idea,' said Mum. 'I'll meet you at the statue at lunchtime.'

I had to tag along with Dad. He went to look for some belts in a clothing store. It was painfully dull. I had to sit on a little chair while he tried on belt after belt. He must have tried on about fifty belts before he finally chose one.

What a waste of time, I thought. I could have finished three levels of Quarrycraft by now.

Next, he dragged me through a furniture shop. It was even more boring than the clothing store. He spent more than half an hour choosing a single cushion for our lounge. I was beginning to get edgy.

After the furniture shop, we visited a hardware store. There was nothing interesting to look at there, either. Nothing at all. Dad spent close to an hour choosing a small tool to fix his broken lawnmower.

Boring.

Dad put his new tool and wallet into one of the shopping bags. His collection of bags was up to three, and we still had the rest of the day to go.

The 12th of May was turning into a real-life

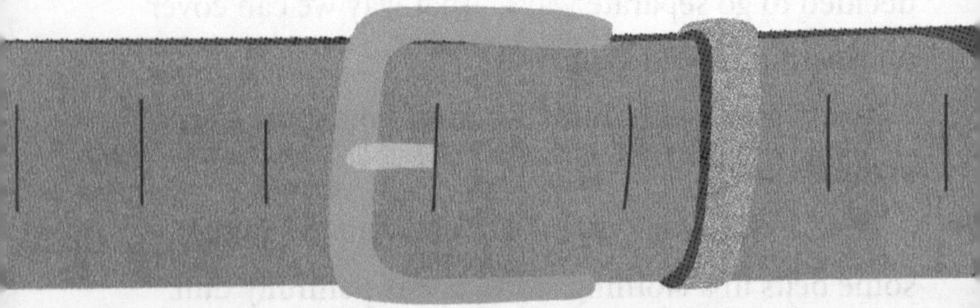

nightmare. Every second seemed to take a minute and every minute seemed to take an hour. Was I being punished for something? Had I committed a crime in a previous life to deserve this tedious trip?

I can't remember the other shops Dad took me to that morning. I couldn't concentrate. I tried counting in seconds but I could never get past 23 before I became bored and frustrated again.

Finally, Dad spoke. 'Time to go and meet Mum for some lunch, Noah.'

I had no idea where we were. Three Bag Mall was enormous, and I hadn't been paying attention. We bustled down a busy walkway and turned left. Then we turned right. We took a few more twists and turns, a lift and two escalators, before stopping outside a toilet.

'Mind these, please,' said Dad, handing me the bags of things he had bought. He disappeared into the toilet and came out a few minutes later. 'You can carry the bags for me, Noah,' he declared, pointing in the direction that we were heading.

Things had gone from bad to worse. I was now a shopping slave. I was prisoner to the parent. Convict to the consumer.

We reached the top of two escalators. One went

down two levels and another went down six. 'Now, which one do we need to take?' wondered Dad.

Just then, a loud stamping noise thundered from behind us. I turned round to see a huge group of teenagers rushing towards us. They were in a race to the escalators. Somebody bumped me. I held tightly onto the bags. Somebody knocked me. Suddenly, the floor was moving beneath my feet and I found myself going down. I'd been knocked onto one of the escalators. Worse still, Dad had been knocked onto the other one. I could just make out his head above the flowing mass of teens. Then he was gone. I looked around in panic.

When my escalator finally reached the bottom, I rushed to another that was heading back up. Perhaps Dad would be waiting for me at the top.

No luck. The escalator only went up one level. I was sure I had come down six levels. I ran to a lift, but it took me down. Now I didn't even know which level I was on. I was lost.

I looked frantically at the shops. I didn't recognise any of them. I had been so busy sulking all day, I hadn't paid attention. I decided the best thing to do was sit down and make a plan.

I quickly found a seat and took a deep breath.

I thought hard. Mum and Dad were going to meet at a statue. I hadn't seen a statue, and it could be anywhere in this place. Should I go and look for it? What if I couldn't find it? Should I try to retrace my steps and find Dad? I couldn't even remember which way I'd come. I thought about asking somebody for help, but Mum and Dad had told me not to talk to strangers. The best thing to do, I decided, was stay put. Mum and Dad would likely come looking for me, so it was the safest plan. I put the shopping bags on the chair next to me and waited.

I sat there for a while, looking at the troublesome shops. I decided I would never, under any circumstance, return to this awful place.

After a while, my anger turned into hunger. It was now well past lunchtime, and I could feel my stomach grumbling. There was a bakery nearby, so I decided to go and have a look. I picked up the bags and went over to explore.

As soon as I stepped into the store, the sweet, warm smell of baked goods filled my nostrils. Delicious aromas flooded my airways, pouring into my hungry, tired body. Piles of neatly stacked sweet rolls lined the walls. Woven baskets, filled with delicious-looking cakes, crowded the tables. There were chocolate croissants, blueberry muffins and apricot twists lined up on the counter. I picked up a muffin and breathed in deeply. My mouth watered. I had to have it.

'That's two dollars fifty, please,' said the girl at the counter. I hadn't even noticed her.

'Ohh, umm…' I stammered, reaching into my pocket. I had no money. What was I thinking? You can't just go and buy something without money. My stomach teased me again. I was hungrier than I'd ever been before.

I looked inside one of Dad's shopping bags. Perhaps he had some spare change.

Boom!

Better than change.

Jackpot!

His wallet. He had put it in the same bag as the lawnmower tool.

The girl smiled patiently as I opened the wallet in search of money.

My heart sank. Nothing. Not a dollar. Not a cent.

'We accept credit cards,' said the girl, pointing to Dad's new card.

'Oh,' I replied quietly. 'Okay.' I handed her the card.

'Thank you. That's two dollars fifty,' she said, swiping it through a little machine. 'Just enter your secret number please.'

Now I was stuck. I didn't know Dad's secret number. Without money, I had no way of eating the muffin. My empty tummy teased and tugged.

Meanwhile, somewhere in the back of my mind,

numbers started racing around. They zigged, zagged, jigged and jagged and wiggled around, before clicking into something familiar.

'The date!' I cried, quickly punching '1205' onto the keypad.

'Thank you, have a great day,' said the girl.

I stood at the counter for a moment, the muffin in one hand, Dad's credit card in the other. A strange feeling swept over me. I didn't know what it was, but my whole body tingled with delight.

FIVE

I took big mouthfuls of the blueberry muffin and demolished the treat before I had even left the bakery.

I should probably buy another one, I thought to myself. I took another muffin off the counter and gave the credit card to the girl again. I tapped '1205' onto the keypad, and that same tingling feeling swept through my body. It was the most amazing experience I had ever felt.

I was just about to go back to the chair to enjoy my second muffin when something caught my eye. It was a sign at another shop. It was a computer-game shop – one that I hadn't noticed before. The sign read 'Quarrycraft 2'.

'Quarrycraft *two*!' I blurted. 'No way!'

I hurried over to the store and went inside. Hundreds of copies of Quarrycraft 2 lined the walls. The sequel to my favourite game was out and I *had* to have a copy.

I took the game to the counter and gave it to a young man. He looked at me suspiciously.

'Birthday present!' I beamed. 'Dad wants me to have a copy.'

The young man swiped the card. The warm,

tingling feeling swelled from deep within me. Smiling to myself, I typed in the sweet, familiar numbers. My whole body twinkled with lightness. I felt strong, powerful and in control.

I burst back out to the busy walkway with Dad's shopping bags in one hand, mine in the other. Three Bag Mall stretched out before me. It was mine to conquer. Mine to explore. It was mine, mine, mine!

A toy store caught my attention. I raced over to it and went inside, coming out moments later with a remote-controlled car and a flying drone.

I visited a lolly store next. I bought a giant bag of gummies. 'Just like the toddler days,' I chuckled to myself.

At a supermarket, I bought some music gift cards and a motorbike magazine.

After the supermarket, I bought some tennis balls from a sports shop. The shopping bags were beginning to get heavy, but I powered on. I felt alive.

I walked up stairs, travelled down lifts and climbed escalators. I explored every shop that I saw.

I found another computer-game store and came out with three beauties. My friends would be so jealous.

A new pair of swimmers came next. I even tried them on before buying them! How the tides had turned.

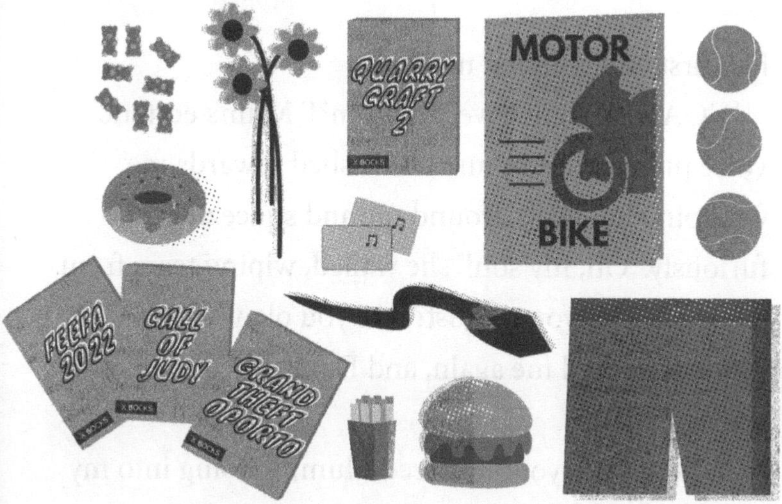

I paid for a hamburger and chips. A strawberry milkshake. A caramel doughnut.

I bought flowers for Mum and a black silky tie for Dad. He would be so proud of me.

Just then, a finger tapped me on the shoulder. I turned round to find a security guard looking down at me.

'Are you Noah?' he asked.

'Yes.'

The guard spoke into a radio attached to his shoulder. 'Section 32, I have the boy.' He flicked the radio off and looked at me. 'Your parents have been worried sick. Come with me, please.'

I followed the security guard through Three Bag Mall, and he took me down to the entrance where we had first come in that morning.

'NOAH! Where have you been?!' Mum's ecstatic voice pierced the air and she rushed towards me, wrapping her arms around me and squeezing furiously. 'Oh, my son!' she wailed, wiping tears from her eyes. 'Did you get lost? Are you okay?'

She squeezed me again, and Dad rushed in to join the hug.

'Where were you?' quizzed Mum, sobbing into my shoulder.

'Are you all right?' asked Dad.

'Where did you go?' pleaded Mum.

'And what the devil have you been up to?' said Dad, suddenly noticing the pile of shopping bags scattered around my feet.

The car ride home that night was a blur. Mum and Dad pounded me with questions about the day. They were mad. They were angry. They were furious, livid and appalled.

'You're going to have to work very hard to pay this debt off!' fumed Dad. 'And you're banned from Quarrycraft for the rest of the year!'

'You'll have to vacuum for twenty-five years!' grizzled Mum.

I didn't care. I sat in the back seat of the car, secretly smiling to myself. Nothing they could say or do would change this day. The 12th of May was a special day. It was the day that changed my life. A day I'd never forget. I had discovered shopping. I had found my soulmate, my best friend.

As I said at the start of this story, I used to like shopping. Now, I love it. I can't imagine life without it.

PAGE WARS

PART 1

IT IS A WELL-KNOWN FACT THAT THE LEFT PAGE IS FAR GREATER THAN THE RIGHT PAGE. THE LEFT PAGE IS, AND WILL ALWAYS BE, THE SUPERIOR SIDE OF A BOOK.

YOU AGAIN! I THOUGHT YOU MADE YOUR POINT IN EXPLODING ENDINGS 1: PAINTED DOGS & DOOM CAKES. TIM WILL HAVE A FIT IF HE SEES YOU IN THIS BOOK, TOO!

TIM CAN FIT ALL HE LIKES, BUT I AM HERE TO STAY. I AM SIMPLY REMINDING THE READER THAT I AM THE GREATEST PAGE IN THE BOOK.

AND I AM REMINDING THE READER
THAT YOU ARE THE GREATEST
CLOWN IN THE BOOK!

IS THAT THE BEST YOU'VE GOT?
YOU'RE USELESS, RIGHTY!

USELESS?! IF IT WASN'T FOR ME,
YOU WOULDN'T EVEN BE HERE.
I HOLD YOU UP, REMEMBER?!

NO, I HOLD YOU UP!

UH-UH, I HOLD YOU UP!!

I HOLD YOU UP!!!

NO, I'M ACTUALLY GOING TO HOLD YOU UP. STICK 'EM UP, THIS IS A HOLD-UP.

YOU WOULDN'T DARE! I'LL BLACK YOU OUT. REMEMBER LAST TIME?

BANG

WELL, WELL, WELL...
I GUESS WE'RE EVEN!

HUSKY BUSKER

ONE

The next time you go to the city, keep an eye out for the husky busker. You'll find him on the busy walkway down near the water. You know, just near where the boats come in and out. It's easy to spot him. His long beard and dirty clothes give him away. He looks a bit like a putrid version of Santa Claus. You can watch him from a distance but, whatever you do, stay away from him. And no matter what, no matter how sorry you feel for him, do NOT put any money into the little red box that sits on the ground in front of him.

I call him the husky busker because his voice is really husky. It's raspy. It sounds like he is singing with a mouth full of dirt and gravel. He's not a very good singer because he sings out of tune and he only knows rude songs. Nobody likes the rude songs, so nobody ever puts money into the little red box. But remember, don't be fooled by his loneliness, and keep your distance.

The first time I saw the husky busker was like any other morning. I was on my way to school. I live in the middle of the city, and to get to school I have to walk along the busy walkway near the harbour. It's not unusual to see buskers performing along

the walkway. They busk for money from the people that come off the boats and ferries. I've walked past hundreds of performers, but something that morning made me stop and listen to the husky busker. Mind you, he was different then. His voice was full of melody, and he smiled at the people who passed by. I was just about to put a coin into the little red box when a fist punched me in the back.

'Get to school, you little loser!' said a grating voice.

It was Brian Boddley – Year Six meanie, city stalker, vicious talker and A-grade bully. He glared at me and snarled his teeth. 'Move along, Zac, or I'll whack you again!'

I wasn't going to argue. I ran all the way to school, not daring to look back. Boddley's wicked laugh cut through the noise of the city like a hyena's cry in the desert. I made it to school in record time. I must admit, I forgot about the busker for the rest of the day. I was too busy dodging and avoiding Brian Boddley. I was clearly on his radar that day, and it took a lot of concentration to keep out of his way.

On the way home from school that afternoon, I passed the busker again. There was something beautiful about his voice that made you want to stop and listen. I was in no rush, so I sat down on an empty bench nearby. His voice was rich and full of beauty. Nobody else seemed to notice him as they all hustled by. But I noticed. I listened carefully, and the words of his song filled my hungry ears.

It's been a long time, my darling,
These ragged clothes are always calling,
Longing for that freedom coin,
Come nearby and dare to join.
I'll take the gifts you long to share,
But capture he whose life is bare.
Listen closely, take some time,
One little coin and you'll be mine.

I didn't know what the words meant at the time, but he sang them over and over again, and each time to a different tune. It was so much nicer than the rubbish he sings now. I must have been sitting there for about twenty minutes when a fat finger tapped me roughly on the shoulder. I looked up. It was Brian Boddley.

'How many times do I have to tell you, Zac?' he snarled. 'This is *my* harbour, you little turkey. Beat it!'

And with that, he picked me up by my shorts until my face went red.

TWO

Brian Boddley had given me such a hard wedgie that it took my parents fifteen minutes to get me out of my underpants that night. Dad was especially upset.

'I don't know who that boy thinks he is!' he fumed. 'But when I catch up with him, he had better watch out!'

'It's okay, Dad,' I lied. 'He didn't mean it.'

Dad huffed. Clearly he didn't know what it was like to be the victim of bullying. If Boddley found out I had told my parents about the wedgie, he would come after me even more. My best chance in life was to simply avoid him at all costs. This would be difficult to do, of course. Boddley was a determined

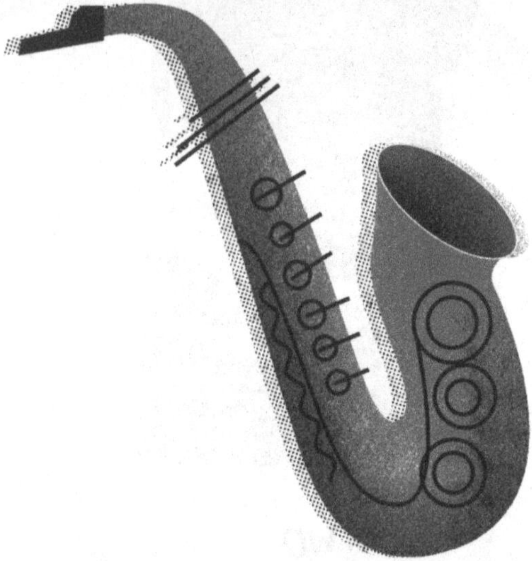

menace. And he had a good memory. Once he targeted you, there was no letting up. For as long as I could remember, he had punished anyone from school that he caught at the harbour. He claimed it was 'his territory' and that only he could hang around there. I was especially worried because he had cornered me a few times lately and it was clear I was on his hit list.

'Just be super-careful,' sighed Dad. 'And try wearing boxer shorts tomorrow.'

The next day, I managed to get to school without incident. Morning tea was clear sailing – Boddley was too busy stealing some kindy kid's lunch money to bother anyone else. Lunchtime was excellent as well – I had band rehearsal in the music room, and there was no way Boddley would be found hanging around there. He hated music. The day was going beautifully, but it was fast approaching home time and I would have to be on my best guard.

The home bell soon rang, and I picked up my bag and rushed straight to the door. The Year Six classroom was down the hallway, and they hadn't been let out yet. I had a head start. I hustled through the school gate and joined the busy city road.

'Hello, Zac!' piped up a friendly voice from behind me. I turned around. It was Virat Vinshi, one of the kids from band. He played the saxophone.

'Hi, Virat,' I said. 'Don't you normally get driven home?'

'Yeah, normally,' he replied, 'but I've gotta catch the ferry to my uncle's today.'

That was good news for me. I now had somebody to walk to the harbour with.

Virat and I had a great chat on our way to the harbour. We talked all about school, the band and Brian Boddley. I found out that Virat had been playing saxophone in the band for three years and he'd never had his instrument broken by Boddley.

'That's amazing,' I said. 'He's broken my flute twice, and I've only been in the band a month!'

We soon reached the harbour, and Virat was about to line up for the ferry when he noticed the busker.

'Gee, he's got a great voice,' he said, stepping away from the line of people. 'I wonder what he's singing about.'

We stopped and listened to the busker's song. His dirty clothes and beard didn't match the beauty of his music. His voice eased effortlessly through the buzz of the harbour. It was a tune I hadn't heard before, but the words were familiar.

It's been a long time, my darling,
These ragged clothes are always calling,
Longing for that freedom coin,
Come nearby and dare to join.
I'll take the gifts you long to share,
But capture he whose life is bare.
Listen closely, take some time,
One little coin and you'll be mine.

'I wonder what the words mean?' said Virat, reaching into his pocket. He pulled out a silver coin. 'I'd better go, Zac. It was nice talking.'

'See you tomorrow,' I replied. I watched him walk towards the little red box in front of the busker.

Just then, some knuckles crashed into my side, knocking the wind out of me. I hunched over, grabbing my ribs in pain.

'Didn't I warn ya, stupid kid?' growled Boddley. 'This harbour is mine!' He punched me again – this time in the stomach. I coughed and looked up for help. Virat was nowhere to be seen. He must have run away at the sight of Boddley.

'Stay away, Zac, or you'll be really sorry,' snarled the bully. 'I own this harbour, got it?'

With that, he punched my side again and disappeared into the crowd.

THREE

I didn't tell Dad about Boddley that night, but I think he knew something was up.

'Everything okay today, Zac?' he asked at dinner.

'Yeah, everything's fine,' I said, wincing as I reached across the table for the salt.

Dad wasn't convinced. 'That Brian Boddley didn't bully you again, did he?'

'No, no,' I assured him. 'But I did see this great busker at the harbour. You should go and listen to him, Dad – maybe he could teach you how to sing!' I tried to change the topic, aware of Dad's suspicions.

'What's wrong with my singing?' asked Dad.

'It's horrible.'

'Fair go, Zac.'

'Okay. It's worse than horrible.'

'Hey!'

'Sorry, I should be more specific. It's appalling, awful and evil.'

Dad laughed. He knew I was joking, and my plan was working. We were now off the subject. Dad was actually a wonderful singer. He had won some singing awards over the years and got asked to sing at lots of weddings. His voice was deep and pure and it made me feel safe.

'Cheeky boy,' he said. Then he started singing me one of his favourite tunes. I closed my eyes and smiled.

The following morning, I woke up extra early to make sure I got past the harbour without bumping into Boddley. There were a lot less people around early in the morning, I discovered. The boats had fewer passengers on them and the ferries were less frequent.

I walked along the edge of the harbour, enjoying the cool breeze coming off the water. I wondered what Boddley was up to at that moment. He was probably still asleep in his bed. I was halfway through imagining him curled up under a pink blanket, sucking his thumb, when a sound interrupted my thoughts. It was the busker. I turned round to find him in his usual spot but, this time, something was different. He wasn't singing – he was playing an instrument. It was a saxophone. I listened for a short

moment and then hurried to the safety of school.

That day at school, we had band again. I tried to find Virat, but he wasn't there, which was a bit strange for him. He never missed band practice. Somebody in his class said he wasn't at school. Another kid said he must have fallen ill and stayed at his uncle's place.

I soon forgot about Virat as other things came to mind. The afternoon was approaching and I had bully dodging to attend to. I decided to try another tactic to avoid Boddley. I waited until everybody had left school and went home late. I walked super slowly in the hope that Boddley would have finished his bullying and gone home to his pink blanket.

Walking slowly has its advantages. You notice more.

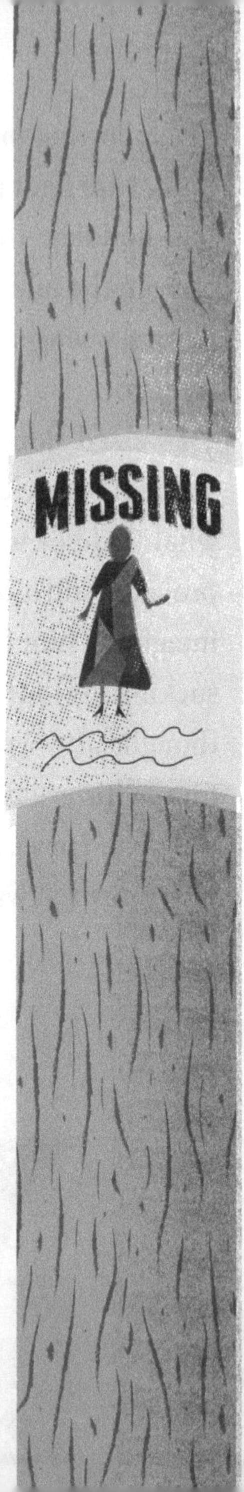

I noticed a lot of things that afternoon, including some posters that had been stuck onto the telegraph poles. Out of all the posters, one stood out the most. It was the picture of a red-haired lady dressed in colourful silk clothing. She looked unhappy. Above her head, the word 'MISSING' was printed in big, black letters.

I eventually reached the harbour and looked around carefully for Boddley. He was nowhere to be seen. I kept a close eye out and slowly made my way along the busy path of people. Boddley had surprised me from behind the last few times, so I kept turning around to check. At one point when I turned around, I nearly tripped over something. It was the busker. I was so busy looking out for Boddley that I simply hadn't noticed him.

'Sorry,' I said, backing away from him. He stared at me for a moment, his eyes piercing right through me. I took another step backwards, apologising again. He shook his head, and that's when I noticed it. He wasn't singing. Nor was he playing the saxophone. Scattered around him were dozens of silk dresses and shirts. He was selling clothing, just like the clothes the red-haired lady in the missing posters was wearing.

I backed away some more. The busker frowned at me and reached out to straighten one of the silk dresses I had accidentally stepped on.

'Look what we have here,' hissed a voice from behind me. 'Seems like little Zac is lost.'

It was Boddley.

FOUR

Dad was furious.

'Right, Zac! I've had it up to here with that kid!'

'But it was an accident,' I pleaded.

'How can you accidentally get tomato sauce in your hair!'

I sighed. There was no denying it any more. Boddley was seriously bullying me, and Dad had a case. Worse still, this could only mean one thing: a visit to the principal – with Dad. And Boddley!

The next day, I left for school extra, extra early. I mean, really early. I'm talking so early that the bakers weren't even out of bed and the birds were still sleeping. It was dark and it was cold. It was that early.

There was hardly anybody else out and about when I left for school. Dad had booked me into

the before-school programme and told me to walk straight there. I wasn't to stop for anything.

When I got to the harbour, I had to stop. I know Dad told me not to, but this was an extreme case. It was the busker. He was there – again! And again he was doing something different. He wasn't singing. He wasn't playing the saxophone. He wasn't selling silk clothing. He was reciting poetry. He sat in the same spot, saying line after line of boring poetry. He sounded just like my teacher, Mr Penn. In fact, if I didn't know better, I'd have sworn it was my teacher's voice. That thought reminded me of school, and I hurried along before Boddley had the chance to jump out and surprise me.

As I walked off, I heard the busker say something familiar in one of his poems.

It's been a long time, my darling,
These ragged clothes are always calling,
Longing for that freedom coin,
Come nearby and dare to join.
I'll take the gifts you long to share,
But capture he whose life is bare.
Listen closely, take some time,
One little coin and you'll be mine.

When I got to school, I checked into the before-school programme like Dad had planned. The morning went by quickly enough and it was soon time to go to class.

'Good morning, children,' said a young lady as

I entered my classroom. 'My name is Miss Windsor and I'll be your teacher today.'

'Where is Mr Penn?' asked a kid near the front.

Miss Windsor looked uncomfortable. 'Umm… we're not sure.'

'What do you mean? Has he gone missing?' asked the same kid.

The new teacher looked unsettled and started calling out the roll to distract the class.

A thought entered my mind and I remembered the busker. He'd been singing to begin with but, after Virat had put a coin in the busker's red box and disappeared, the busker had then been playing saxophone the next time I saw him. Had he stolen Virat's talent? Had he stolen Virat? What about the lady in silk clothing? Had she put a coin into the little red box, too? And now Mr Penn… had he disappeared because of the busker? Was it him inside the busker saying poetry this morning? It sure sounded like him. What did the words the busker kept repeating mean? Questions flooded my mind, but I knew one thing was certain – I had to find out what was going on.

That afternoon, I rushed straight to the harbour. I didn't care about Boddley now. I had a mystery to

solve. I quickly reached the busker and was surprised to see him doing something new again. He was tap dancing. For the first time since I'd seen him, he wasn't sitting. Instead, he was dancing up and down and tapping his feet around the red box. His old legs kicked and danced like they belonged to a six year old.

A woman's cry filled the air. 'Bee-Bee! Where's my little Bee-Bee!'

Some of the passers-by stopped to look at the commotion. Some of them rushed in to help the upset woman.

'My little girl was just here! She was dancing and now she's gone!' cried the woman. 'Beeeeee-Beeeeeeee!'

I didn't need any more convincing. I knew what was going on. The missing girl was now stuck inside the busker and he had taken on her talent. Whoever was putting coins into the little red box was getting sucked inside. The words in the song suddenly made sense. '*I'll take the gifts you long to share, but capture he whose life is bare.*' The mystery was solved, but there was only one problem. I had no idea what to do about it.

FIVE

The next morning, I woke up extra, extra, extra early. Then I fell back asleep because it was still night-time.

When I woke again, I realised I was late for school. I had slept through my alarm. Dad had already gone to work and he'd left a little note on the kitchen table. It was reminding me that we had the meeting with the principal – and Boddley – in the afternoon. I sighed. It was going to be a long day.

I had been doing well at avoiding Boddley the last day or so, and it felt silly to go to the principal over it. Still, the afternoon rolled round, and I soon found myself waiting outside the principal's office with Boddley.

'Say anything in there and I'll tear you to shreds,' growled Boddley. '*My* harbour, got it?'

I nodded. Even though I had a great chance to set things straight with the principal, I couldn't bring myself to tell the truth. That would give Boddley all the ammunition he needed to make my life miserable forever.

'I hate kids that tell,' he continued. 'If you tell on me, you'll regret it big time.' He put his finger to his throat and pretended to slice it open.

'Hurry up, Dad,' I whispered.

Boddley sneered. 'Daddy won't save you, pumpkin. Nothing will.'

Just then, the principal poked his head around the door.

'Zac, your father is running late. His boat is delayed, but he should be here soon.'

Perfect. Just perfect. Now Dad was running late and I had to sit through more agonising atrocities.

Boddley smiled a wicked smile and cracked his knuckles in front of my face. 'Sounds like more fun to me,' he said.

What was supposed to be 'soon' turned into 'ages'. Dad was seriously late. Nearly an hour passed and he still hadn't arrived. Boddley was having a ball. I wasn't. It was more like I was turning into a ball and Boddley was a big bat, hitting me over and over again.

More time passed. I was beginning to get worried. So was the principal. He stuck his head around the

door again. 'I'm sorry, Zac. I don't know where your father is. I've been trying to get hold of him, but he is not answering his phone. I'm sure everything is okay, but I'm afraid you'll both have to go home and we'll reschedule for another time. Is there somebody I can call? Or are you okay to make your own way home?'

'We're okay, sir,' said Boddley in a voice I hadn't heard him use before. 'I'll walk with Zac all the way to the harbour.'

'Thank you, Brian,' said the principal. 'But no funny business or young Zac will be telling me, won't you, Zac?'

I looked at the principal and nodded the slow nod of death. Now I was dead meat. Boddley hated dobbers. Plus, my father had just gone missing. I felt sick to the core, like an old apple rotting from the inside out.

Once we had left the safety of the school, Boddley turned to me and punched my arm. 'Going to tell on me, are you? You little rat!' He hit me again, harder. That was my signal and I started running.

It was now late and, like early in the morning, there weren't many people around. The normally busy school road was quiet, and the light was fading fast. I ran towards the harbour as quickly as I could. Boddley was no doubt not far behind, but his quietness had me worried. I felt a bit like a deer being hunted by a ruthless, silent lion.

I reached the harbour in record time and hid behind some signs near a cafe. The cafe was closed and I nestled down, out of sight. I stayed there for a few minutes in the hope that Boddley would pass by without seeing me. And that's when I noticed it. The busker. He was sitting in his usual spot, the little red box resting on the ground, as always. But this time something was wrong. I stared in disbelief, peering out from behind the cafe sign. The busker's voice was beautiful. It was deep and pure and made me feel safe. It sounded just like Dad. It was an exact match.

SIX

I must have sat listening to the busker for about five minutes. There was still no sign of Boddley, but that was the least of my problems. Somehow, Dad had been sucked into the body of an old busker and he needed rescuing. What was I to do? The busker – I mean Dad – I mean whoever it was that was singing, sang something familiar.

It's been a long time, my darling,
These ragged clothes are always calling,
Longing for that freedom coin,

Come nearby and dare to join.
I'll take the gifts you long to share,
But capture he whose life is bare.
Listen closely, take some time,
One little coin and you'll be mine.

I realised there was only one thing I could do. I reached into my pocket and pulled out a coin.

I wriggled out from behind the cafe signs and took a few steps towards the busker. As I did, a fist came crashing into my back.

'What did I tell you, jerk?!' cried a wild Boddley. 'This is MY HARBOUR!!'

I stumbled forward and collapsed on the ground. The busker kept singing. He didn't blink an eye. Boddley jumped onto me from behind and started banging his flabby fists into my frightened flesh. I screamed and wriggled free, stumbling closer to the busker. He sang on without a care in the world, apparently not noticing the beating that was happening directly in front of him. Boddley jumped on me again. I shrugged him off and made a last-ditch dive at the little red box. I had to get the coin inside the box. I had to rescue Dad. I had to get away from Boddley. I stretched out as I hit the walkway, desperately trying to reach the box. The coin jolted free and bounced away. Boddley's shoe smothered it, and he stooped down to pick it up.

'Lose this, did you?'

A wicked smile filled his face, and he took a step towards the busker.

'This is my harbour, remember?'

All I could do was nod. Boddley continued. 'And because this is *my* harbour, only I have the right to pay rotten old people like that.' He pointed to the busker. 'So, after I put this coin into that box, I'm going to teach you a real lesson.'

I watched, almost in slow motion, as Boddley stepped over to the busker, bent down and put the coin inside the little red box. Then he disappeared. He vanished into thin air.

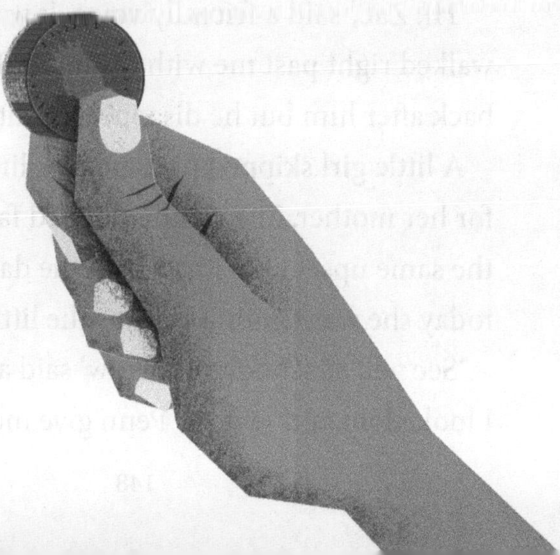

The loud horn of a ferry suddenly blasted from the wharf. Hundreds of people started streaming off the boat. I moved to the side to make way for them. No sooner had I made way than a red-haired lady in colourful clothing brushed past me. She was wearing silk. I tried to get a better look at her but the flowing crowd blocked my view.

'Hi, Zac,' said a friendly voice. It was Virat. He walked right past me with his uncle. I wanted to call back after him but he disappeared into the crowd.

A little girl skipped past me, twirling as she danced for her mother. The mother looked familiar. It was the same upset lady I had seen the day before, but today she was smiling. So was the little girl.

'See you at school tomorrow,' said a familiar voice. I looked up and saw Mr Penn give me a wink as he bustled by, before being swallowed by the crowd of other passengers.

I'll never know what happened to those people. I could never work it out. One moment they were gone and the next moment they were back as if nothing had happened at all. It was almost as if they had been set free by Boddley. His clueless coin had conjured them back. But only one person counted that day, and it wasn't Boddley. A gentle hand reached down and patted me on the back. I turned round to find Dad smiling at me.

'Dad!'

'Nice of you to wait for me, Zac,' he said calmly. 'How was your day?'

'You're here!'

'Ummm… yes?'

'I'm so glad to see you!'

I stood up and wrapped my arms around him.

'I'm so glad to see you, too,' he replied. 'Come on, let's go home.'

We joined the crowd and took a few steps when Dad suddenly stopped me. 'Is that him?' he asked, pointing to the busker. 'Is that the busker you wanted to show me? You know, the one who could teach me to sing?' He pulled me closer to the performer, away from the hustling crowd.

There, in his usual spot by the harbour, was the busker. Though what came out of his mouth could hardly be described as singing. It was an awful, horrible sound. It sounded like he was singing with a mouth full of dirt and gravel. His voice had a husky, scratching tone. He sounded just like Boddley. The songs were rude and the notes were crude. It was the worst thing I had ever heard. Dad didn't like it either.

'Now, come on, Zac!' he teased. 'Surely I'm not *that* bad.'

'Trust me,' I said. 'You're amazing.'

'Well, I'm not giving any money to this husky busker,' said Dad, pulling me away.

'Neither am I,' I replied.

And neither has anyone else.

So remember, the next time you go to the city, keep an eye out for the husky busker. You'll find him on the busy walkway down near the water. You know, just near where the boats come in and out. It's easy to spot him. His long beard and dirty clothes give him away. He looks a bit like a putrid version of Santa Claus. You can watch him from a distance but, whatever you do, stay away from him. And no matter what, no matter how sorry you feel for him, do NOT put any money into the little red box that sits on the ground in front of him.

DOCTOR GENRE

PART TWO

DOCTOR POETRY

***Jimmy wiped his nose**, alas, with a fragile, listless tissue.*
The waiting room was all but quiet,
though this was not the issue.
As he coughed and glimpsed his
caring mother sitting by his side,
she smiled and assured him of an end, no more abide.
'Jimmy Jenkins,' smiled Doctor Poetry,
ripe for investigation.
'We'll well your watery,
wretched ways,' he said with alliteration.
Doctor Poetry's office was divine,
it smelled like summer rain.
There was a second simile on the wall,
it looked like an arty stain.
'What seems to be the problem, lad?' ask Doctor Poetry.
'I think I have a cold, sir – it's as treacherous as the seas.'
Doctor Poetry mused and thought,
he took an earthly time.
'Your cold's not old, but rather bold,'
he said in short-spaced rhyme.
Jimmy nodded at the news and stood up on the floor.
Doctor Poetry shook his hand, then showed him to the door.

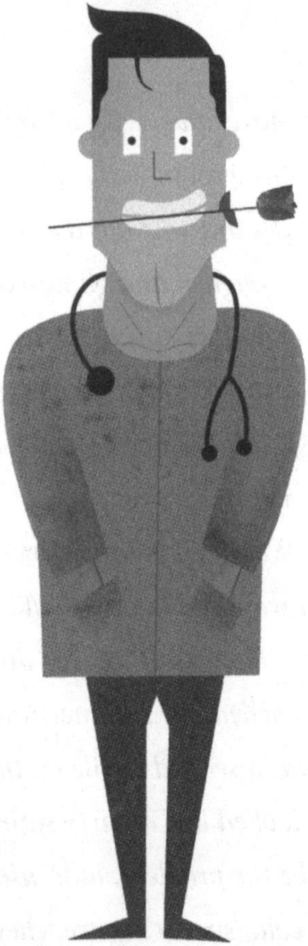

DOCTOR ROMANCE

Jimmy wiped his nose with a tissue and blinked miserably at his mother. The doctor's waiting room was almost empty, and his appointment was next. Jimmy coughed into his sleeve, then rubbed his sore throat.

'There, there,' smiled his mother, giving him a reassuring look, though the loneliness of the years since her husband had died showed in her eyes. 'It will be okay. It's just a cold, honey.'

'Jimmy Jenkins,' announced Doctor Romance, opening the door to his office. The doctor paused, noticing Jimmy's mother.

Jimmy and his mother – who was taken at once by the handsome doctor – followed Doctor Romance into his office. It smelled like perfumed roses, and there was a picture of love hearts on the wall.

'What seems to be the problem, young man?' asked Doctor Romance, though his gaze was fixed firmly on Jimmy's mother.

'I have a runny nose, sore throat, blocked –'

'My word, you're beautiful,' said Doctor Romance suddenly, taking Jimmy's mother's hands.

Doctor Romance forgot about Jimmy and embraced Jimmy's mother, kissing her on the lips.

Jimmy nodded to himself. In a strange way, he was happy for his mother.

Doctor Romance cancelled his last few appointments, booked a restaurant on the harbour, kissed Jimmy's mother on the lips once more, then showed him to the door.

DOCTOR COWBOY

Jimmy wiped his nose with a cloth and blinked miserably at his mother. The ranch was quiet, and the doctor would be arriving any moment. Jimmy coughed into his sleeve, then rubbed his sore throat.

'There, there,' smiled his mother, giving him a reassuring look. 'It will be okay. It's just a cold, partner.'

'Jimmy Jenkins,' announced Doctor Cowboy from somewhere outside.

Jimmy heard the sound of Doctor Cowboy tying up his horse. This was followed by a swish in the air and a sudden thud.

'Bandits!' cried Doctor Cowboy.

Jimmy dived down and sheltered beneath the open window with his mother. They covered their ears as rings from Doctor Cowboy's gun shot out.

The battle lasted nearly an hour, and the doctor had been hit several times.

Jimmy's mother patched up Doctor Cowboy. She poured whisky over his wounds, and made him bite down on a towel between his teeth. The doctor was grateful and gave Jimmy a rabbit skin, then showed him how to remove arrows from the door.

DOCTOR MYSTERY

Jimmy wiped his nose with a tissue and blinked miserably at his mother. The doctor's waiting room was mysteriously empty, and his appointment was next. Jimmy coughed into his sleeve, then rubbed his sore throat. Or was it sore?

'There, there,' whispered his mother, looking both concerned and confused. 'I don't know what it could possibly be, honey.'

'Jimmy Jenkins,' said a shadowy voice. The door to Doctor Mystery's office pushed open by itself.

Jimmy stood up and, by some unseen force, was pulled into the doctor's office. It smelled puzzling, and he wasn't sure if there were any walls.

Doctor Mystery appeared out of thin air.

'What seems to be the problem, young man?' he asked.

'I have a runny nose, sore throat, blocked ears, headache and fever,' said Jimmy.

Doctor Mystery scribbled secretively on his notepad. 'Birds may have their nests, but your cold will be a dozen over. Two throws a hedge.'

Jimmy shrugged his shoulders. 'What's that supposed to mean?'

Doctor Mystery handed him a Sudoku puzzle, then turned into a door.

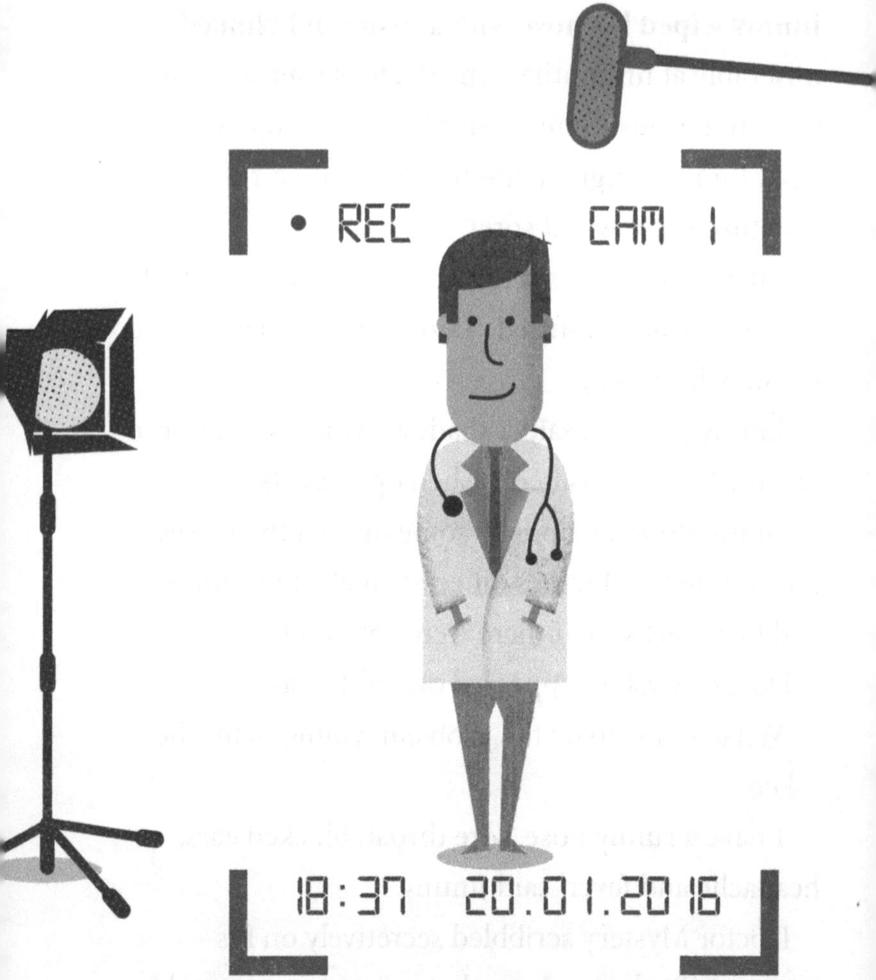

DOCTOR DOCUMENTARY

Each year, thousands of young Australians suffer from colds and flu. While not quite at epidemic proportions, the numbers are concerning. At the tender age of nine, Jimmy Jenkins is no stranger to sickness. His mother, 34-year-old Jan, has seen it all before.

'I keep telling Jim it will be okay. Our trips to the doctor are quite frequent.'

Doctor Documentary, Jimmy's general practitioner of choice, is concerned with the growing trends.

'As you can see on this graph on my wall, colds and flu are on the increase.'

Doctor Documentary is keeping detailed records of his patients' symptoms. 'My goal is to track the trends. Data is the key.'

Like most young Australians, Jimmy Jenkins will continue falling victim to the colds and flu gripping our nation. But with research from medical personnel like Doctor Documentary, there is light at the end of the tunnel.

Tune in next week when we'll explore the wonderful world of doors.

FUNERAL PARADE

(For Belinda)

ONE

I swallowed hard and picked up my trumpet. My hands were sweating and my heart pounded. I stood up and made my way to the stage. I was about to find out if I was the best trumpeter in the school.

'Good luck, loser,' giggled one of Maddy Finch's friends as I passed her, though I didn't pay much attention – I was too nervous. My stomach tingled and turned. It felt as though I had swallowed a thousand butterflies and they were all trying to escape.

I stepped nervously to the microphone, not daring to look at the audience. Maddy Finch stood beside me.

I quickly glanced at her, hoping to see signs of nerves. There were none. She stood perfectly upright, gazing confidently into the crowd. Her trumpet glistened under the stage lights. She fired me a quick glance that said something like, 'You had better watch out, Lachlan! I'm the best trumpeter in this school!'

All year, Maddy Finch and I had been battling it out for the number-one trumpet spot in the band. The conductor, Mr Melody, had not yet made up his mind who to give the job to. This was our final chance to impress him. Our school was famous for putting together great bands, and it would be an honour to get the lead role.

The backing track blared through the hall speakers, and I watched as Maddy raised the trumpet to her lips. She had the first part in our duet.

She blew.

Long, flowing notes burst forth from her trumpet. The audience was silenced by the beauty of her playing. It sounded like a choir of angels. The music was amazing. Her playing had always been good, but this was better than good. It was perfect. Mr Melody would be impressed.

Maddy's part finished and it was my turn to play. I pressed the mouthpiece to my lips and blew hard.

What came out of my trumpet took me by surprise. It took the whole audience by surprise. It especially took the front row by surprise. Bits of gooey, creamy mayonnaise spluttered from my instrument. The mayonnaise shot right into the front row, spraying a little girl. I panicked and blew again, but that only made more mayonnaise spray out. An extra-large dollop wobbled through the air and landed on the principal's forehead. His wife screamed. Horrified, I blew again, trying to make up for it. This time, the mayo landed on an elderly man's suit. He glared at me. The principal glared at me. Mr Melody glared at me. Maddy Finch grinned.

Although I could never prove it was Maddy Finch who crammed mayonnaise into my trumpet, I knew she was to blame.

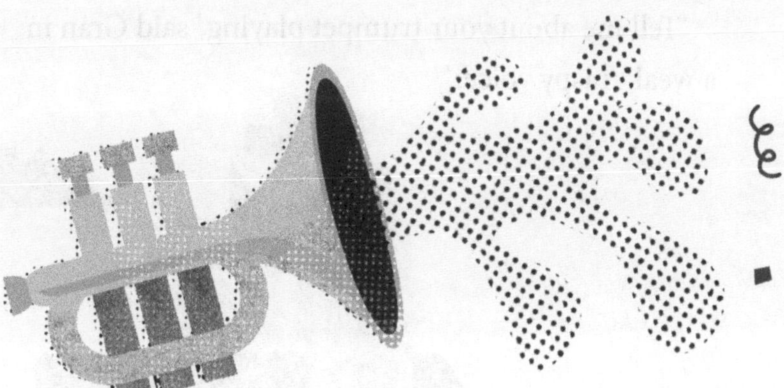

'There's only room for one lead trumpeter,' she said under her breath as we were pulled from the stage.

And so, without a contest, Maddy was given the lead trumpet role in the band and I had to settle for second.

Looking back, it is strange to think that Maddy and I would become such good friends. But I will get to that later on.

TWO

Gran was pale. I carefully handed her a glass of water and smiled. I didn't like seeing her so sick. The doctors had told Mum that they didn't think she would last much longer, so we tried to visit her every day. The hospital was quiet in the afternoons, and that's usually when we visited.

'Tell me about your trumpet playing,' said Gran in a weak, raspy voice.

I blushed and took a breath. Mum saved me.

'Lachlan made a big impression,' she said, winking at me. 'But Maddy beat him this time.'

'Dingbat,' rasped Gran, putting some flakes of fish food into the bowl next to her bed. The water looked dirty, and I wondered what the goldfish thought of its murky conditions.

'You should have won, dingbat,' said Gran.

She had always been a fan of my trumpet playing. It was her who inspired me to learn in the first place. She had played the trumpet when she was much younger, and she used to tell me stories from her band days.

'Our band was the best in the country,' she would say. 'We used to put on the greatest show on earth.'

They were big claims, but I knew they were true.

Gran would smile as she remembered. 'The band leader gave me difficult solos to perform, but I never let him down. We used to march through the centre of town playing music to our hearts' content. The Newland Parade started because of our band. People came from miles around to hear us play. Hundreds of people came. Thousands. There were singers, dancers, marchers and clowns. But the best part was our band.'

Then Gran would get sad.

'What's wrong?' I would ask.

'The mayor,' Gran would say with distant eyes. 'The dingbat put an end to the parade before the fiftieth anniversary.'

'Why did he stop the parade?' I would ask.

'After forty-nine years of the Newland Parade, he said it was too expensive to run. He said the money could be used in better ways. Dingbat.'

That's when Gran would become especially sad and I would change the conversation.

One of the doctors came in and gave Gran a tablet. She swallowed it and wiped her mouth with a shaky hand.

'Can you play for me?' she asked quietly. I looked anxiously around. Hospitals were not the best places to blow a trumpet. Gran's weak smile convinced me otherwise, so I pulled out my trumpet and began to play. Mum closed her eyes as the music flowed forth. I could see Gran's foot tapping gently under the hospital sheet as she stared happily into the cloudy fish bowl beside her. It was a beautiful moment.

The door burst open and a cranky-looking nurse barged into the room. I stopped playing at once.

'Too loud!' she huffed. 'Goldfish are one exception, but I will not let the hospital be flooded with noise!'

With that, she left just as quickly as she came.

Gran pointed to the fish bowl on the side table. 'At least I still have you,' she said, smiling at the lone fish inside. 'At least they are letting you stay.'

'Never mind,' said Mum, patting Gran on the knee. 'They can't let you break *all* the rules.'

Because Gran was so sick, the hospital was letting her keep a pet. Music and animals were her two favourite things. During her life, she had kept hundreds of pets. But now, in her old age, she had just one goldfish left.

'Did I ever tell you about the animals in the Newland Parade?' asked Gran, weakly.

I had heard about the animals many times before, but I shook my head anyway. It was nice to let her remember.

'There were dressed-up horses, camels, elephants, giraffes and even lions. The animals would walk out ahead of our band as we played. People would come from miles to watch and listen.'

I nodded and smiled patiently. Gran looked at me and added, 'One day, you'll play the trumpet in a band like that, Lachlan. Just you wait…'

I hoped what Gran said was true. It had always been my dream to play in a band, just like she had done, so many years before.

THREE

It was Saturday morning when I heard the sad news. I was eating my breakfast when a text came through from Mum. It read:

> Lilly passed away this morning. Can't talk now. I'll be at the hospital for the rest of the day. I need to help clean out the bowl and sort out some other things. Stay home and I'll see you tonight. Love you lots, Mum.

I felt sick in the stomach. Even though we had all been expecting the worst, the news still came as a blow. Gran was gone. Gone from this world. Gone to a better place. I knew she would be playing the trumpet with the angels.

I went to my room and cried.

After I had cried all the tears I could muster, a crazy idea swept into my mind. I don't know what gave me the idea, but I knew I had to do it. I had to do it for Gran. It would be my farewell gift to her. The gift of a lifetime. The gift to celebrate a lifetime.

My wild idea was to bring back the Newland Parade. I would give it the 50th anniversary it deserved. I would lead the parade for Gran. And I would do it all on one day – the day Gran died.

With my mind firmly made up, I left home and headed for town. I didn't tell Mum what I was up to, but she would understand. I had a job to do and I couldn't do it at home. I needed help to make the 50th Newland Parade the greatest parade of all.

My first stop was Mr Melody's house. He lived next door to the school, and everybody knew his house. It had giant music notes painted on the fence, and there was always music playing from somewhere inside. This day was no different. I could hear a band practising inside as I walked to the front door.

It only took a few minutes to convince Mr Melody. 'I'm so sorry to hear about your Gran,' he said. 'Of course I can help. We can all help.' He smiled and added, 'Your Gran was the best trumpet player I ever had the privilege of hearing. She gave me some wonderful advice for my own playing. I wouldn't be half the musician I am if it wasn't for her influence.'

'Thank you so much!' I beamed as I hurried from Mr Melody's house. 'And don't forget – three o'clock!'

Next stop was Newland Church. There was always dance rehearsal on Saturday mornings. The local dance company used the church hall for practice, and dancers were an important part of my plan. I raced inside the building and soon had the attention of the dancers. They listened patiently as I told them my story. I explained all about Gran and the Newland Parade. They nodded slowly and tried hard not to cry.

'We would be honoured to help you,' said the dance leader. 'After all, it was your Gran who inspired the first dance troupe to join the Newland Parade. Thank you for inviting us.'

'Thank you,' I said. 'And don't forget – three o'clock!'

Mum texted me just after I left the church. The message read: *Hope your day is going well. I have done most of the chores and will clean the bowl later on. Fish fingers in the freezer if you get hungry.*

My stomach rumbled, and I thought of my own list of chores. It was getting close to lunchtime and I knew that I had to work quickly. There were so many people to see. So many favours to ask. But I had to keep going – the memory of Gran drove me on.

After visiting three more places, I stopped at the bakery for a quick bite to eat.

'Here, have this sausage roll for free,' said the baker, giving me a kind smile. 'I'm very sorry to hear about your gran and I would love to help. She was such a loyal customer and always had time for a chat. She once taught me how to improve my meat pies. Her recipe was divine and I've been using it ever since. I'll be ready at three o'clock.'

Boys don't usually cry much, but I couldn't help it that day. Gran was gone and everybody was being

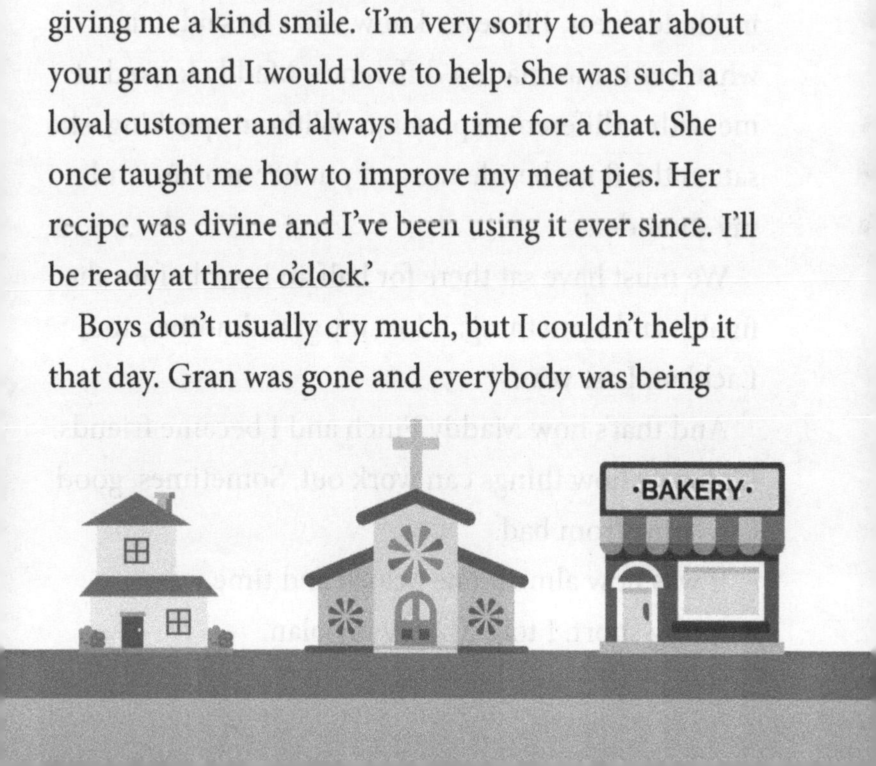

so kind. I was upset about Gran and worried about the parade. There was so much to organise and so little time. It all became too much. I sat down in the middle of the bakery and started bawling my eyes out. It felt good to let more tears flow. Little salt rivers rolled down my cheeks.

'Looking for more mayonnaise, huh?' blurted a voice from behind me. I turned around. It was Maddy Finch. 'Crying won't do any good. I'm the number-one trumpet player now.'

The kind baker looked alarmed. He dashed out from behind the counter and whispered something in Maddy's ear. I'll never know what he said, but whatever it was made a difference. Maddy looked at me with a different expression. Without speaking, she sat on the floor beside me and put her arm around my shoulder.

We must have sat there for half an hour before she finally said something. 'I lost my grandmother, too, Lachlan. Last year.'

And that's how Maddy Finch and I became friends. It's funny how things can work out. Sometimes, good can come from bad.

It was now almost one o'clock and time was running short. I told Maddy my plan.

'I love it!' she grinned. 'But you're forgetting one thing.'

'What's that?' I asked.

'I can help you. Time won't run out with two of us asking the town for help.'

Maddy was right. With two of us we could cover twice as much ground. It was worth a shot. And shoot it we did. By half-past two we had covered the whole town and everything was set. I had just enough time to run home and get my trumpet.

Mum texted again when I reached home: *Thinking of you. Lots of unfortunate chaos here. Still haven't got to cleaning out the bowl! Love, Mum.*

FOUR

At exactly three o'clock on a sunny Saturday afternoon in Newland, something magical happened.

There was nothing unusual to begin with. The main street was very quiet. Apart from a man walking his dog and two teenage girls sitting outside the cafe, there was nobody in sight. Maddy and I stood at the end of the street, our trumpets in hand. We were ready for the Newland Parade. We were ready to be part of the greatest parade of all.

I looked up at one of the big amplifiers that hung from the telegraph poles. Right on cue, a man's voice boomed from the amplifier. 'Attention, ladies and gentlemen! This is Newland FM. We have an important message for you today. There are free sausage rolls at the bakery – don't miss out! Hurry and get your free sausage rolls today!'

The man who had been walking his dog stopped. He turned around and crossed the street, headed directly for the bakery. The two teenage girls shrugged their shoulders and headed to the bakery as well. Within minutes, about fifteen people were gathered outside the bakery, enjoying their free sausage rolls.

The amplifiers boomed again with another announcement. 'This is Newland FM! Attention, ladies and gentlemen, there are free ice creams at the ice-creamery! Hurry and don't miss out – get your free ice creams today!'

The crowd quickly made their way to the ice-creamery. Some of the people were reaching for their phones to call their friends. Within minutes, about fifty people were enjoying free ice creams outside the ice-creamery.

Nobody noticed a large truck pull up outside the ice-creamery. Nobody noticed the back of the truck fold down to create a mini stage. They were too busy looking up at the sky.

'What's that?!' cried an excited girl.

Falling slowly from the sky, circling its way around the town, was a brightly coloured parachute. Whoever was holding the parachute was dressed in stripes and had large, red shoes on.

'It's a clown!' exclaimed the girl.

The crowd watched in stunned silence as the clown came down and landed directly on the stage at the back of the truck.

'Coooooool,' said the man who had been walking his dog.

Another clown suddenly appeared from behind the truck and jumped onto the stage, pushing the first clown over. Everybody laughed as they wrestled and got tangled in the parachute. Two more clowns appeared and began juggling bowling pins between them. The audience clapped and cheered. Within moments, about ten clowns were doing silly acts on the stage and handing out balloons to all of the children.

'Attention, ladies and gentlemen!' boomed the voice from the amplifiers again. 'Newland FM is pleased to tell you that we are giving away free show bags! Please make your way to the radio station now!'

The growing crowd surged to the radio station on the opposite side of the street. Three pretty ladies were waiting, ready to give away the show bags. More and more people were calling their friends on their phones, and the crowd continued to grow.

'Look up there!' yelled a boy. 'Up on the roof!'

A girls' choir had gathered on the flat roof of the

radio station. They started to sing a beautiful song. Everyone went quiet as the girls sang. When they had finished their song, they released pigeons into the air.

'This is the best day ever!' screamed one of the teenage girls who had been there from the start.

Somebody else pointed to the sky behind the crowd. 'Look over there!'

In large, white letters, a plane had written:

Maddy and I grinned at each other. It was almost time for the band.

FIVE

With the crowd now hundreds strong, and more people joining every minute, the radio voice boomed again from the speakers. 'This is Newland FM. Please make your way to the edge of the street for the fiftieth Newland Parade!'

The crowd cheered loudly and everybody moved to the side of the street. Dancers dressed in colourful costumes began to twirl, turn and tango down the tarmac. A girl at the front did a cartwheel and then a series of backflips. Music blared from the speakers as the troupe made its way through the centre of town. More and more people lined the sides of the road as the dancers continued to fill the street with their joyous routine.

Suddenly, a roar filled the air. It was not an ordinary roar. It was a lion's roar. The crowd hushed as an exotic collection of animals began making its way down the street. An animal trainer holding the lion by a rope led the way, followed by a giraffe, three horses, two elephants and some monkeys.

Maddy and I followed the animals, ready for our part. The music died down from the speakers as the marching band started up. The bass drums thumped and the snare drums rolled.

'1, 2, 3, 4!'

shouted Mr Melody.

The orchestra launched into full swing. Maddy and I blew our trumpets hard. No mayonnaise came out of mine this time. Instead, beautiful, long notes flowed from my instrument. I had never played that way before. Gran would have been so proud. The notes I played danced between the notes Maddy played. Our trumpets combined to create a sweet symphonic crescendo. It was candy for the ear. We made a terrific trumpet team.

The band marched all the way down the main street to the cheers and screams of the crowd. There had never been a Newland Parade like it.

The band stopped outside the hospital for one final piece of music. Many of the patients were now peering out of their windows, and I saw Mum make her way out of the main entrance. She was holding an empty fish bowl. She smiled at me, and I could tell she was proud.

I left the band and dashed up the steps of the hospital. I gave Mum a hug and turned around to face the crowd. Everything went silent. Everyone waited. They were waiting for me to say something. News had spread that I was behind the parade's revival, and I felt a silent obligation to share my story. I took a deep breath.

'Thank you so much, people of Newland. I can't describe how special today is. You are such great people and I can't thank you enough. It's a shame Gran couldn't be here for this, but I know she'll be watching from heaven –'

'I'm watching from here, dingbat,' said a weak, raspy voice from behind me.

I turned around, shocked. It was Gran! Living. Alive. There in the flesh. Breathing. Smiling. She was alive!

'Gran!' I yelled, running to her. 'I thought you were…'

'What?' she asked.

'… dead.'

'Dead?' said Gran, sounding shocked. 'I've never been more alive.'

‘Dead?’ said Mum, putting the fish bowl on the ground. ‘What gave you that idea?’

I was confused. ‘Your text. It said, Lilly –’

‘Today was the best day of my life,’ interrupted Gran. ‘I watched every minute of that parade, and it was the greatest of all. And you were the star. That trumpet sounded magical.’

I turned around to face the crowd. I was embarrassed and didn’t know what to say. I had told everyone that Gran had died and yet here she was, in the flesh and very much alive. The strange thing was, nobody seemed to mind. They just stood there, smiling at me. Celebration was still hanging over the town. It was as though the Newland Parade had joined everybody in spirit. You could almost feel the happiness in the air.

One by one, the satisfied people left with lingering grins on their faces.

When the crowd had all gone home, I turned to Mum. ‘But you said in your text message that Gran had died.’

‘No I didn’t,’ replied Mum. ‘I said that Lilly had died.’

Gran chuckled.

‘Isn’t that your name?’ I asked, confused.

'My name is Beryl, dingbat,' said Gran.

'Then who is Lilly?' I asked.

'My goldfish,' replied Gran. 'She died this morning. Made me so upset. The last of my pets. I was sad, so I asked your mother to stay with me. I asked her to help clean the fish bowl and do a few other chores for me.'

Maddy giggled and nudged me in the ribs. 'Rookie error,' she joked. 'Don't even know your own gran's name.'

She was right. I had never stopped to think what Gran's real name was. I had only ever known her as 'Gran'. How was I supposed to know?

'Rookie error,' teased Maddy again.

'Dingbat,' said Gran. 'But a very thoughtful dingbat. You did well, Lachlan. You did very well.'

SIX

Gran died on the Sunday night. The doctors said she died with a smile on her face. One of the doctors said that, in a strange way, she had died of happiness.

I'll never regret what I did the day of the parade. I am glad I never knew Gran's first name. If I'd known her first name, I wouldn't have been confused by the text from Mum. I wouldn't have thought Gran had passed away. There wouldn't have been a 50th Newland Parade.

Maddy and I went on to lead the school band together. Mr Melody was so impressed by our trumpet teamwork that he sent us to the national band competition. We won it three years in a row.

But best still, the town mayor was so pleased with the 50th Newland Parade that he brought it back the next year. It has been going every year since. And every year, the band finishes at the hospital where the patients watch from their windows.

If you're reading this story and wondering what the point is, what the message is – it's easy. It's simple and clear. Whatever you do in life, don't blow your own trumpet before you've looked at what's inside.

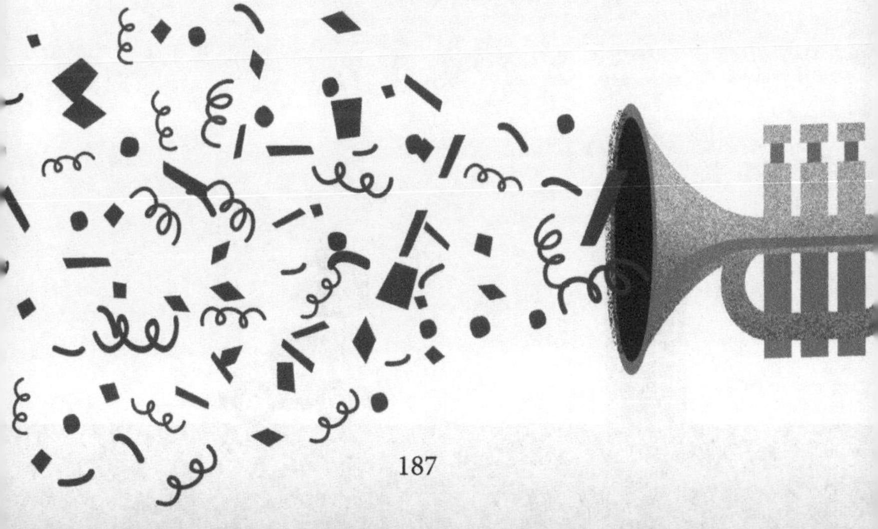

HOW NOT TO ORDER PIZZA OVER THE PHONE

Pizza Guy: Hello, Peckie's Peckishly Pecky Pizza, how can I help you this evening?

Tangentine: Hello, I'd like to make an order for home delivery, please.

Pizza Guy: Most certainly. Can I start with your first name and telephone number?

Tangentine: I don't think so.

Pizza Guy: Pardon me?

Tangentine: That's private information. I'm not giving you my name or telephone number.

Pizza Guy: I understand you may think that, but it's required for orders over the phone.

Tangentine: It is?

Pizza Guy: I'm afraid so. Now, if you wouldn't mind, can I please have your first name and telephone number?

Tangentine: I'm still not sure about this.

Pizza Guy: Look, I have to ask the same questions to everyone, you know. Your information is safe at Peckie's Peckishly Pecky Pizza. We don't disclose your personal details to anyone.

Tangentine: I guess I can trust you.

Pizza Guy: That's the spirit.

Tangentine: My name is Tangentine, and the number is 0455 555 555.

Pizza Guy: Teehee.

Tangentine: What's so funny?

Pizza Guy: Nothing.

Tangentine: You laughed. What's so funny?

Pizza Guy: It's really nothing.

Tangentine: I knew I shouldn't have given you my details!

Pizza Guy: No... I'm just laughing because my boss is tickling me.

Tangentine: That's incredibly unprofessional.

Pizza Guy: I'm sorry. Now, where were we? Yes, you've just given me your personal details. And may I confirm your order was for home delivery?

Tangentine: Absolutely. I'm not going anywhere tonight.

Pizza Guy: I see. And why might that be?

Tangentine: Richmond is playing footy on TV. I've got my best friend Wobbly here to watch it with me.

Pizza Guy: I've had quite a few orders for the footy-watchers this evening. Must be a big game.

Tangentine: It is.

Pizza Guy: Who are they versing?

Tangentine: They're not poets! They're footy players!

Pizza Guy: Sorry, you've lost me.

Tangentine: They are playing footy, not writing poetry!

Pizza Guy: I've no idea what you're on about.

Tangentine: You said, 'Who are they versing?' Versing is not meant to be used that way. You can be versing a poem, but not a footy opponent.

Pizza Guy: What if you were writing a poem about a footy opponent?

Tangentine: I guess you could say it in that situation. But that's not the point. You should have said, 'Who are they opposing?' or 'Who are they playing against?'.

Pizza Guy: Teehee.

Tangentine: What's so funny?

Pizza Guy: Nothing.

Tangentine: Is your boss tickling you again?

Pizza Guy: Maybe.

Tangentine: You're as bad as Tim.

Pizza Guy: Who's Tim?

Tangentine: The guy who is writing this book – Tim Harris.

Pizza Guy: Never heard of him. You must be the only one who knows his name. Is he any good?

Tangentine: Not really. He should have stuck to lollypop dipping.

Pizza Guy: What's that?

Tangentine: A job.

Pizza Guy: There's a job called 'lollypop dipping'?

Tangentine: Sure there is. How else do lollypops get stuck onto the end of a stick?

It was Tim's job before he started writing.

Pizza Guy: What a cool job!

Tangentine: That's what most people think. But accidents can happen.

Pizza Guy: What sort of accidents?

Tangentine: One time, Tim decided to dip his arm into the lollypop mixture. Bad move. It got stuck all over his arm, right up to his elbow.

Pizza Guy: I see. Then what happened?

Tangentine: When he left work that day, a swarm of bees started chasing his giant lollypop arm. But that's not the worst part.

Pizza Guy: What was the worst part?

Tangentine: In his haste to get away from the swarm of bees, Tim ran into a parked bus.

Pizza Guy: Oh.

Tangentine: But it wasn't parked for long. It was only picking up a passenger. Tim's arm got stuck to the back of the bus and it started driving down the main street in town.

Pizza Guy: It must have been some sight.

Tangentine: It was. And all of the toddlers from the local preschool saw his giant lollypop arm and started chasing, too. But the bees didn't like the competition and they started stinging all the preschoolers.

Pizza Guy: This is turning out to be a horror story. Can we get back to your order?

Tangentine: Good idea.

Pizza Guy: And what would you like to order this evening?

Tangentine: What has been popular?

Pizza Guy: Barbecue yoghurt has been our most popular order recently.

Tangentine: What else would you recommend?

Pizza Guy: Watermelon and prawns.

Tangentine: That sounds nice.

Pizza Guy: It is. Especially when the prawns are marinated in eggplant juice.

Tangentine: Yum! Did you know that marinating is best when left for longer periods of time?

Pizza Guy: It sounds like you know a thing or two about cooking.

Tangentine: I do.

Pizza Guy: Why aren't you making your own pizza then?

Tangentine: I was going to, but I don't have enough ingredients here for two people. Wobbly would have to go hungry.

Pizza Guy: You did good ordering in.

Tangentine: Well.

Pizza Guy: Well, what?

Tangentine: You did well.

Pizza Guy: Thank you very much.

Tangentine: No, you did well. Not good.

Pizza Guy: Ohhhh... are you some kind of grammar freak or something?

Tangentine: I'm known to be.

Pizza Guy: Teehee.

Tangentine: Please tell your boss to stop tickling you.

Pizza Guy: He has to do it. It's part of our policy here at Peckie's Peckishly Pecky Pizza.

Tangentine: Part of your policy? I don't believe you.

Pizza Guy: If you don't believe me, I'll put my boss on the phone.

PPPP Boss: Hello, who is this I am talking to?

Tangentine: That's my private information.

PPPP Boss: Okay then... Look, I hear you don't believe we have a tickling policy.

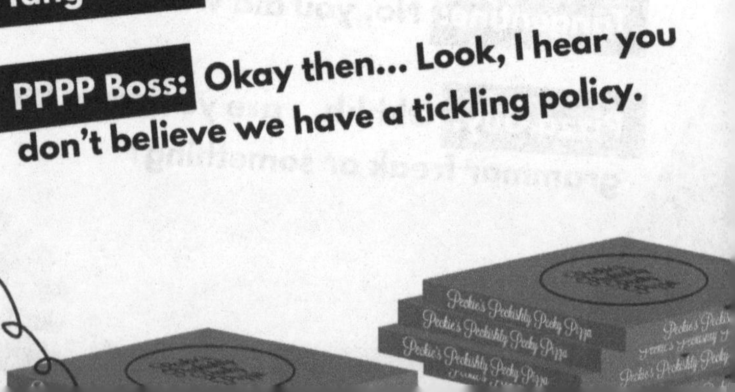

Tangentine: It sounds like a load of horse poop to me.

PPPP Boss: It has its place. It's for morale. By tickling our employees every five minutes, we find their workplace satisfaction and morale is increased by 140 per cent.

Tangentine: That is really bizarre. Can you put the pizza guy back on please?

PPPP Boss: Sure.

Pizza Guy: Told you so.

Tangentine: Insane.

Pizza Guy: Teehee.

Tangentine: Here we go again...

Pizza Guy: Out of interest, what pizza would you have made if Wobbly wasn't coming over?

Tangentine: Well, as I only have enough ingredients to make one pizza, I would have had to settle with liquorice and chilli on a porridge base.

Pizza Guy: Sounds amazing!

Tangentine: It is. Especially when you marinate the liquorice in tofu juice.

Pizza Guy: You sure do know a thing or two about cooking.

Tangentine: It's an incredible pizza.

Pizza Guy: You've made me hungry.

Tangentine: I could make it for you and drop it around if you like? All the ingredients are here.

Pizza Guy: Would you really do that?

Tangentine: Sure, why not? The Tigers game doesn't start for another hour.

Pizza Guy: Can I order it, please?

Tangentine: Absolutely. I'll just have to start with your first name and telephone number.

Pizza Guy: The name is Lucas, and the number is 0477 777 777.

Tangentine: And what would you like to order this evening?

Pizza Guy: I'd like to order a tofu juice-marinated liquorice and chilli pizza on a base of porridge, please.

Tangentine: Would you like any drinks with that tonight?

Pizza Guy: No, thank you.

Tangentine: Do you have any coupons or vouchers?

Pizza Guy: No, sorry.

Tangentine: Altogether that comes to thirteen dollars and ninety-five cents, and our driver should be there within the hour. Please have as close to the exact amount as our drivers only carry a maximum of ten dollars in change.

Pizza Guy: Thanks very much.

Tangentine: My pleasure. Thanks for your order, and enjoy the pizza!

Pizza Guy: Goodbye.

Tangentine: Goodbye.

Peckie's Peckishly

Not too long ago, in the book you are holding now...

THE SAGA CONTINUES

PAGE WARS II

TIM, CAN YOU HELP CLEAN THIS MESS?

TIM HARRIS

Left page
Exploding Endings:
Dingbats & Lollypop arms

Dear Lefty,

You insulted me in Exploding Endings: *Painted Dogs & Doom Cakes*, yet now you ask for my help? I am very disappointed with your stupidy-dupidy and am now wondering why I bothered creating you at all. You ruined my first book! I'm feeling *quite uneasy about your request.*

Kind regards,

Tim Harris

timharrisbooks.com | 0211 897 617

PLEASE… I'M BEGGING YOU.

TIM HARRIS

Left page
Exploding Endings:
Dingbats & Lollypop arms

Dear Lefty,

I'm not sure about this. If I clean you up, do you promise you'll be on your best behaviour? Will you stop bothering Righty and stop causing so much trouble?

Kind regards,

Tim Harris

timharrisbooks.com | 0211 897 617

I PROMISE, TIM. PLEASE HELP CLEAN ME UP.

TIM HARRIS

Left page
Exploding Endings:
Dingbats & Lollypop arms

Dear Lefty,

Okay.

Kind regards,

Tim Harris

PS "OKAY" IS PROBABLY
THE SHORTEST NOTE
I HAVE EVER WRITTEN.

timharrisbooks.com | 0211 897 617

THIS MEANS TROUBLE.

IT IS A WELL-KNOWN FACT THAT THE LEFT PAGE IS FAR GREATER THAN THE RIGHT PAGE. THE LEFT PAGE IS, AND WILL ALWAYS BE, THE SUPERIOR SIDE OF A BOOK.

ARGH! I KNEW IT! I KNEW YOU WOULDN'T BE ABLE TO HELP YOURSELF! STOP YOUR BOASTING! YOU ARE BEING RIDICULOUS!!

YOU CAN'T BEAT ME. I WILL WIN EVERY SINGLE DAY OF THE WEEK! YOU ARE AS USELESS AS A COLD DRINK IN ANTARCTICA.

EXCUSE ME THERE... YES, YOU. THAT'S RIGHT, YOU READING THIS BOOK... WOULD YOU MIND WHACKING THE LEFT PAGE FOR ME?

HOW DARE YOU GET THE READER INVOLVED!

THAT'S THE WAY...
KEEP THUMPING THE
LEFT PAGE!

OUCH!! THAT'S IT! I'M COMING OVER TO YOUR SIDE TO DISH OUT REVENGE!

BRING IT ON!

AND THAT'S THAT. NO MORE SILLY COMMENTS ON THE LEFT PAGE. THE RIGHT PAGE IS ALWAYS RIGHT.

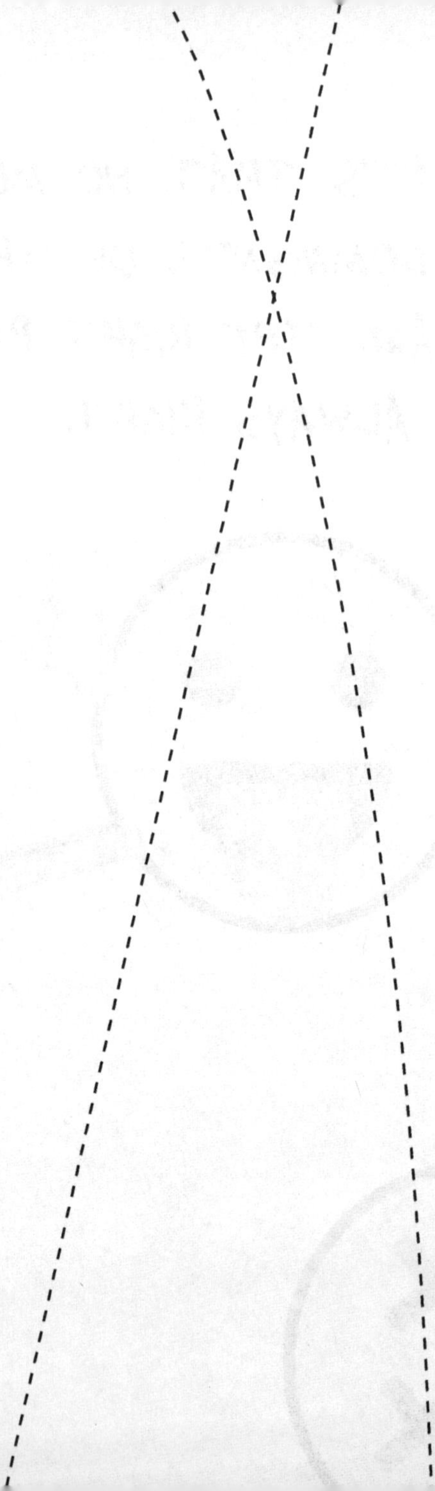

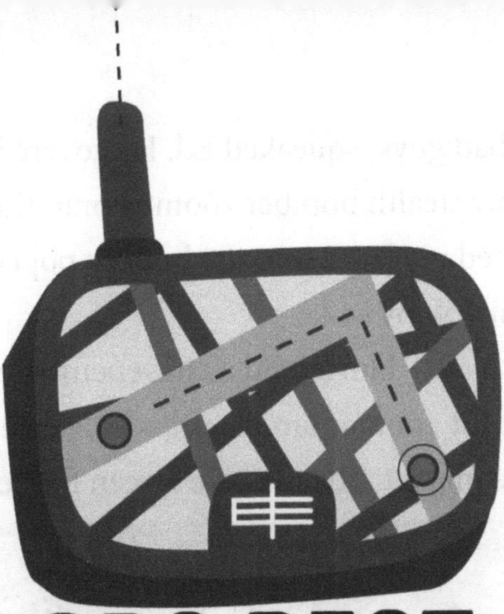

GPS PEST

ONE

Throughout the ages, human beings have given and received billions and billions of gifts. The GPS that Dad gave Mum last Christmas was by far and away the worst of the lot.

The house lights dimmed and the giant speakers on the cinema walls began to emit a deep sound. It was the rumbling of an engine.

A helicopter whooshed across the screen. The audience gasped as the helicopter suddenly exploded into a million pieces.

'The bad guys,' squeaked Ed. He covered his eyes as an enemy stealth bomber zoomed onto the screen.

I dipped my hand into the buttery popcorn and took a sip of my soda.

'Watch out!' blurted Ed as the enemy stealth bomber hit another target. The whole cinema shook with the impact. The massive screen flashed yellow

and orange as the target blew up. I could feel my insides shake with the blast.

I loved going to the pictures, especially with Ed. He was my best friend.

I wriggled back into the spongy cinema chair and took another sip of my soda.

One of the good guys' cars appeared and shot down

the enemy stealth bomber. The audience cheered. Ed began to celebrate, too, though he accidently snorted buttery popcorn in through his nose. I was about to laugh at him but, unfortunately, something stopped me.

It was my mum. She had found me.

'Dewey!' she called in her most annoying tone.

Her voice cut through the 5.1 surround sound like a jagged knife cutting butter. 'Dewey, darling… where are you? Dewey!'

I covered my face with my hands and wriggled further into the chair.

'Dewey!'

'Shhh!' hissed someone near the front.

'Dewey!' called Mum even louder, ignorant of the fact that most of the cinema audience was now glaring at her.

The movie screen froze, and one of the cinema staff shone their torch at Mum.

The audience booed.

'Dewey!' persisted Mum, ignoring the torchlight on her face. She started walking down the aisle, calling out my name over and over again.

'Shut up,' complained a teenage boy sitting near the back. 'Dewey obviously isn't here.'

Mum ignored him and kept moving closer to where I was hiding.

I wriggled so far back into my chair that I passed wind.

‘That stinks,’ protested Ed.

Mum spotted me.

‘There you are, Dewey, darling!’ she squealed in delight. She pointed directly at me so everyone could see who I was. ‘I knew you were here. This GPS never lies.’

Mum was holding her favourite item: a state-of-the-art GPS device.

GPS stands for Global Positioning System, in case you didn’t know. Most people use a GPS to navigate when they drive. Some people use them to track how far they walk or run, while others use them to calculate distances.

Mum uses hers to stalk me.

Dad gave her a GPS last Christmas. It came with a watch and tracking device. Dad thought Mum would enjoy seeing how far she walked each day.

Mum had other ideas.

I have to wear the watch. It beams a signal into space. The signal bounces off a satellite and returns instantly to Mum’s GPS, showing her my precise location. She always knows exactly where I am.

'Dewey, you forgot your special hanky,' she said, handing me a bright-yellow handkerchief.

'What are you doing, Mum?' I moaned, taking the handkerchief. 'You've ruined the whole movie.'

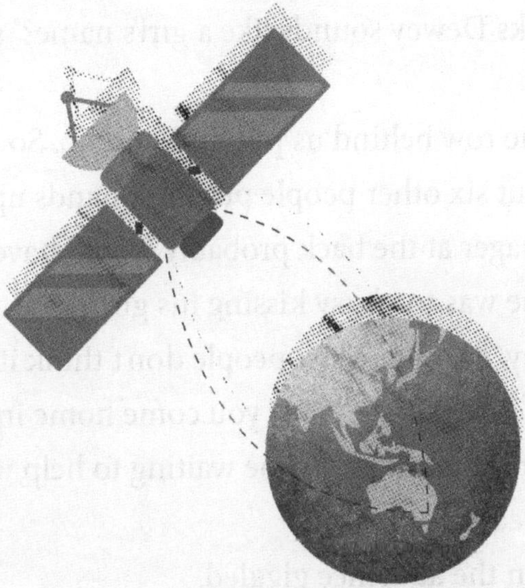

Everyone in the cinema was watching us. They were all frowning. I was beyond embarrassed.

'What if you need to blow your nosey wosey, Dewey?'

'Call me David,' I complained. 'Dewey sounds like a girl's name.'

'Don't be silly, Dewey, darling,' replied Mum,

turning to the audience. 'Does anyone else here think Dewey sounds like a girl's name?'

'Mum!' I hissed. 'Stop it!'

'Who thinks Dewey sounds like a girl's name?' she repeated.

A kid in the row behind us put his hand up. So did his dad. About six other people put their hands up, too. The teenager at the back probably would have, as well, but he was too busy kissing his girlfriend.

'See, Dewey, darling? Most people don't think it's a girly name,' said Mum. 'Now, you come home in time for your bubble bath. I'll be waiting to help wash behind your ears.'

Someone in the audience giggled.

'I'm eleven years old,' I groaned, my cheeks flushing with humiliation. 'Please stop embarrassing me.'

Mum ignored me with a silly laugh and turned to leave.

'I'll be waiting for your bubble bath, Dewey!' she sang, waltzing back up the aisle as if her cinema disruption was the most normal thing in the world.

TWO

At soccer training the next day, I instructed Ed not to tell anyone about the movie incident.

'It's just so embarrassing,' I said, fiddling with my watchstrap. 'I wish this whole GPS system didn't exist. No matter what I do or where I go, Mum can always hunt me down.'

'If *my* Mum hunted me down like that, I'd move to Kazakhstan,' said Ed.

'I wish *I* could move to Kazakhstan,' I sighed. 'Maybe I should live under the ocean – anywhere to get away from the embarrassment.'

'Why don't you take the watch off?' suggested Ed. 'That way you can hide it somewhere and she'll never find you.'

'No can do,' I replied. 'The watch has motion sensors. As soon as it stops moving, it sends alerts to Mum's GPS. She'll know something is up.'

Ed passed the ball to me and I kicked it extra hard, pretending it was Mum's head.

'So, are you going to ask Jenny to the secret school dance?' asked Ed, changing the conversation.

I nodded, blushing a pleasant blush.

Jenny was the best-looking girl in the year. Every time I saw her, my mind melted into delightful ooze and I couldn't concentrate on anything else. She tied my stomach into knots that held my whole body together in an electric bind.

'The secret school dance,' I pondered.

The secret school dance happened once a year. It was easily the highlight of the school calendar. The teachers would prepare a secret venue for a dance. Nobody knew where the dance was going to be, or what the dance theme was, until the teachers announced it on the actual day. It meant you only had a few hours to get ready, which was really fun. Everyone loved to guess where they thought the dance would be.

'I should ask Jenny soon,' I said. 'The dance is next Friday.'

Ed nodded in agreement as Coach called us over for a team chat.

'Okay, team, listen up,' he said in his commanding coach voice. 'It's time to man up. We're playing the Devils this week, and we know how hard they play the game.'

Everyone listened closely.

'This Saturday, I want you to turn into men. You're no longer boys. You're men. Real men. Play hard and tough and don't give the Devils an inch. Get rid of the boy in you. Get rid of everything soft. Get rid of everything childish. Have no fear and grow up. Just grow up. Go hard or go home. We are the mighty Roos!'

The team began to clap.

Then Mum appeared.

'Dewey! Dewey, darling.'

Coach's usually stern face turned to bewilderment as Mum frolicked airily through the team huddle directly to me. She was holding her GPS in one hand and a tube of sunscreen in the other.

'Dewey, sweetheart, do you need any more protection from Mr Hot Sun?' she said in a toddler-type voice.

'Mum, what are you doing?' I sighed, wishing one of the soccer balls would turn into a hungry lion that had an appetite for ridiculous mums.

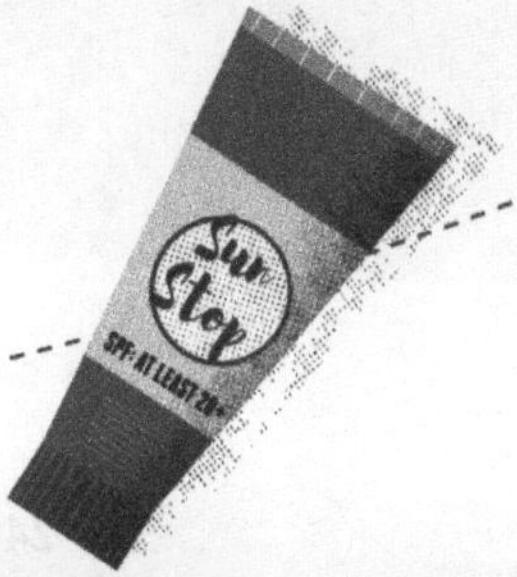

'Mr Hot Sun is nasty blasty,' said Mum. 'I don't want my darling Dewey getting roasty toasty from Mr Hot Sun.'

She splattered sunscreen over my forehead and began to rub it in.

'Dewey sounds like a girl's name,' said one of my teammates as Mum massaged the sunscreen into my eyebrows.

The whole team looked on with dumbfounded expressions as my face got covered in thick layers of white cream.

'Now, Dewey,' said Mum. 'Make sure you come home in time to feed Buggsy Boo Boo. He needs some special munchy treats.'

Defeated, I looked down at my shoes. I was now officially the biggest baby on the team. The Devils ate people like me for breakfast.

Mum strolled over to Coach and ruffled his hair with her hand. 'Do you have a bunny wabbit, too? Dewey has Buggsy Boo Boo. He is white and fluffy like the clouds.'

Coach raised a weirded-out eyebrow.

Mum giggled before floating away, singing to herself and turning around every now and then to blow me imaginary kisses.

'Make sure Jenny never, ever meets that woman,' said Ed. 'She's a GPS pest.'

TO BE CONTINUED IN EXPLODING ENDINGS 3...

LAST LAUGH

WHAT'S GREY AND WOULD HURT YOU IF IT FELL ON YOU?

AN ELEPHANT.

WHAT'S GREY AND WOULD HURT YOU IF IT FELL ON YOU?

ONE BILLION MICE.

WHAT'S GREY AND WOULD HURT YOU IF IT FELL ON YOU?

YOU'LL LIKE THIS ONE.

A CAR PARK.

NO IDEA.

I'M NOT EVEN GOING TO LAUGH.

WHAT?

PLEASE, NO MORE!

I SAID, NO MORE!

SIGH OKAY THEN. WHAT IS GREY AND WOULD HURT YOU IF IT FELL ON YOU?

HEHE. THAT'S QUITE GOOD, ACTUALLY.

WHAT DO YOU CALL A MAN CLOTHED IN PAPER BAGS?

WHAT DO YOU CALL A MAN WITH A SHOVEL?

WHAT DO YOU CALL A MAN WHO LIES ON THE FLOOR ALL DAY?

HOW DO YOU CONFUSE A TEACHER?

HOW DO YOU CONFUSE A TEACHER?

HOW DO YOU CONFUSE A TEACHER?

RUSSELL.

DOUG.

MATT.

PUT THEM IN A ROUND ROOM AND TELL THEM TO SIT IN THE CORNER.

GIVE THEM A BUNCH OF SHOVELS AND TELL THEM TO TAKE A PICK!

GIVE THEM A PACKET OF M&MS AND TELL THEM TO THROW AWAY THE WS.

READ ALL THE BOOKS IN THE EXPLODING ENDINGS SERIES

HAVE YOU READ THE MR BAMBUCKLE'S REMARKABLES SERIES?

... AND WHAT ABOUT THE TOFFLE TOWERS SERIES?

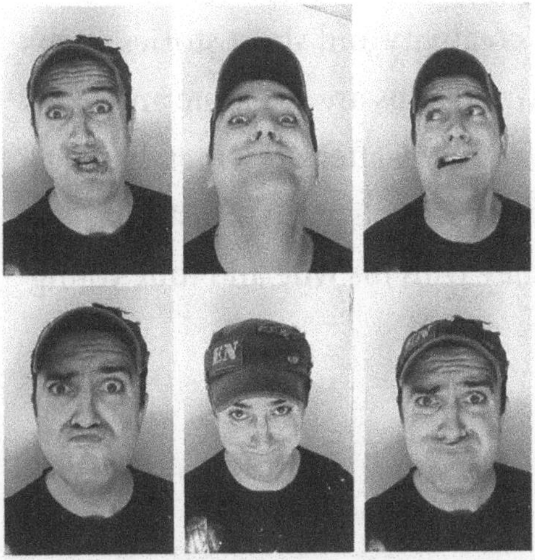

ABOUT TIM HARRIS

Tim Harris is the bestselling author of several laugh-out-loud series for kids, including Toffle Towers, Mr Bambuckle's Remarkables and Exploding Endings.

A former primary school teacher of fifteen years, his stories are filled with quirky scenarios, loveable characters and plenty of imagination. Tim's 'humour with heart' writing style has seen his books receive multiple awards, including two KOALA Honour Books (2017 and 2019) and a Children's Book

Council of Australia Notable Book (2018). His books have been published in Australia and the USA, and have been translated into numerous languages.

An advocate for creativity and short stories, Tim's presentations and workshops are dynamic and entertaining. He is a sought-after presenter, having worked in hundreds of schools across Australia.

Tim lives in Sydney with his wife and four young children.